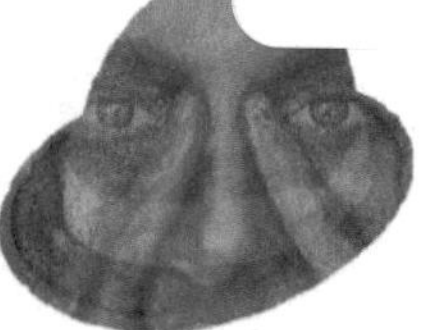

Creative Hats

First published in Great Britain, 2023 by C H Press, a division of Creative Hats.

First published in Hertfordshire in 2023 by C H Books, an imprint of Creative Hats Press.

This paperback edition published in 2023. Copyright © Fantastic Writers, 2023

Cover design by: C H Books

Edited by: Lewis Green

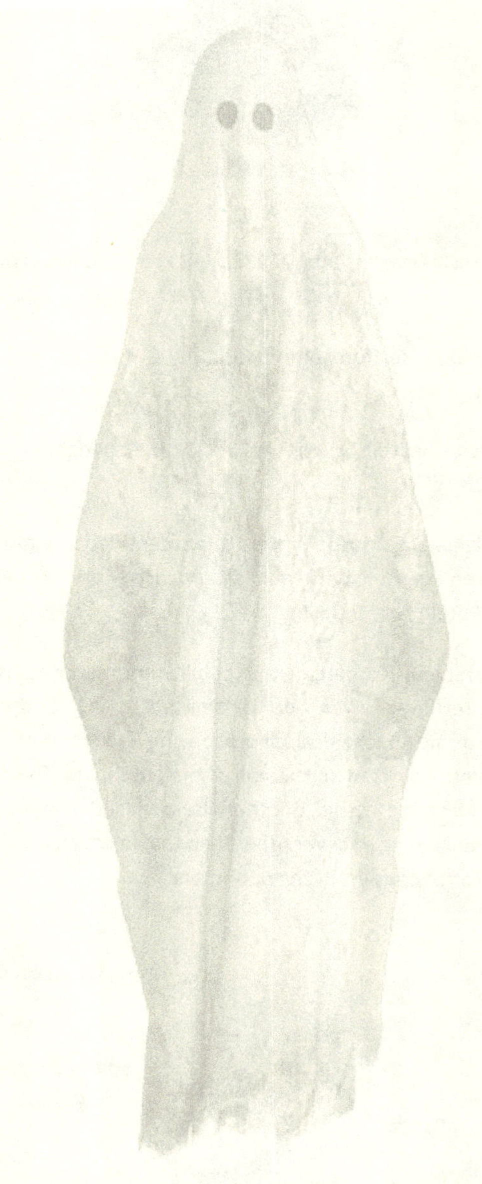

Contents

Martyn Kempson

Go quickly and fetch

Help from the priest

Or the exorcist

So as to avoid

The terror of the ghoul.

*Hitchin photo courtesy of Kelly Hatley

(Historical context)

The Headless Horseman

by Julie Dawson

A cavalier called Goring to Highdown House did ride.

Pursued by Cromwell's army, wanting a place to hide.

He hid inside an elm tree to wait for their retreat

But when he was discovered, his heart it skipped a beat.

> On the fifteenth of June when the moon shines bright,
>
> the headless ghost goes riding into the summer night.
>
> From Pirton on his white horse to Hitchin he will fly.
>
> This man will be a legend, his ghost will never die.

"Oh, you cavalier you've made a great mistake.

We've come to take your life and you cannot escape!"

With one fell swoop they caught him and butchered off his head.

A piercing scream ran through the air as Goring fell down dead.

> On the fifteenth of June when the moon shines bright,
>
> the headless ghost goes riding into the summer night.
>
> From Pirton on his white horse to Hitchin he will fly.
>
> This man will be a legend, his ghost will never die.

Watching from a window was a lady all in grey.

When she saw her sweetheart slaughtered, she could no longer stay.

She escaped to Hitchin Priory and hid within the walls.

Her ghost now walks about the grounds on a moonlit June nightfall.

On the fifteenth of June when the moon shines bright,

the headless ghost goes riding into the summer night.

From Pirton on his white horse to Hitchin he will fly.

This man will be a legend, his ghost will never die.

L.J. Green

Haunted

Of course I did. Of course I did. I knew she was the one from the very first moment I saw her. I knew it by the play of early morning light that danced across her still-closed eyelids. I knew it by the way she laughed, shyly at first as if she wasn't sure if I was in fact joking, and then when she knew that I was, until she couldn't stop. I knew it by the way she would hum to herself as she got dressed in the morning. I knew it by the way she would catch my eye and then look quickly away as if she had been caught out in some children's game. Or by the way she would brush against me as she walked past, and then hurry away giggling. But most of all I knew it by the way she rested her head on my chest when I was weighed down with whatever the day had brought me; politics, religion, morality – it all weighed heavily on me in those days.

I first saw her when I was living at High Down sometime during the autumn of 1650. She was here doing her maids training and was soon to start working at the nearby Priory Hotel. It was here of course that we would regularly meet after our acquaintance had been made. But enough about that for now.

It has been so long since peacetime in this once green land, now pock-marked with cannon and musket-fire, scorched, scarred and sorry. We had been stationed here at High Down on confidential orders delivered straight from the hand of King Charles himself. This was before of course, at Whitehall, his head rolled and came to rest finally at his twitching feet. I did not attend the execution myself but know of many who did. They tell me a moan of such that had never been heard before went up from the crowd as the executioner's sword found its mark. What a country has been created that the crowd saw fit to dip their handkerchiefs in the spilled blood of our king! After the king's murder, our mission became more important than ever. We were to engage in espionage and gather intelligence against the Roundhead stronghold in the neighbouring towns. Straight into the viper's nest as it were. Trained as I was, it was still not a prospect I was looking forward to. But then, as I said, I met her.

She was at High Down for her maids training amongst a group of eight or nine others. I came down for breakfast one day and walked straight into a viper's nest of another sort. I was the first one down, as was how I liked to start my day, and walking into the dining room I was surprised by the appearance of so many maids and those training them. Upon my entrance their conversation immediately ceased, and I felt the unease of having so many pairs of eyes bear down upon me.

"Coffee sir?" Her eyes gleamed with something akin to mischief and I couldn't help but smile.

Hers was the first face to greet me every day that week, a week in which her first words to me that day were simply: "*Coffee sir?*" And somehow, those two words were enough. And so, day by day, our flirtations grew, became bolder, became something more.

Whoever said prayer doesn't work? She was assigned to clean my room and I could tell just by looking, the extra care she had taken when turning down my sheets, the care that had gone into the simplest of tasks, to make the mundane well, less mundane. The first thing I would do upon coming back to my room in the evening was to hold a pillow to my face so that I could better smell the scent of her perfume. I also found freshly cut flowers in the vase every day. Tell me then, if this is not love, what is it?

By January her training was complete, and she and the other maids were sent back to the care of the Priory Hotel. Now; politics, religion, morality, love. This hardly served to ease my burden. But our story is not finished here.

I missed her intently from the very start and I would mope around the corridors and gardens of High Down for days on end. Now, you could say, why didn't I just follow her to the Priory Hotel, knowing it as well as I did. But, knowing it as well as I did meant that I knew that the area was swarming with Roundheads and was thus an extremely compromising position for me. But to stay away from her was hellish, and I could not abide to do so for very long. And so, I began to plot and ponder, how to meet her and to maintain my cover. And maintaining one's covertness is not an easy proposition either. I had risen quickly through the ranks and was proud of the position I had attained. This I missed the most – riding my horse through the streets, my scarlet sash sitting proudly on my chest. This I would no longer be able to do. At least not for the time being.

And so, daily I would walk to the Priory Hotel in the clothes of a not-quite-commoner, but also, nothing that would set me apart from any regular business owner. As soon as she first saw me in the dining room of the Priory, a smile spread across her face, and did I detect a slight blush rise to her cheeks? Yes, I believe I did. Initially I stayed for two nights on 'urgent business' and ensured she overheard the number of the room in which I was staying. That three-hour wait was the most anxious that I have ever endured. But eventually there came a rapping at the door, a rapping so soft that it could only have come from her. I won't bore you with the details of what next passed between us, but I will leave it to your imaginations. From that point onwards that became our routine every other day and every day in between our meetings was lost to tedium and anxiousness, and these days moved so slowly it was as if I had been suspended in time. My visits to the Priory were also fruitful in other regards. It was here that we were able to gather useful intelligence on the Roundhead contingent, their movements, their meeting places, their methods. And so, this continued until the middle of June, my travelling between the Priory and High Down. When my assignment was to end in August, we were to leave this place and be married. This we had discussed many times and we both had a desire to live by the sea.

It couldn't last of course. My friends and I, we were betrayed. By whom, we never found out. She had a day off and she had come to stay with me at High Down for the afternoon. We had earlier enjoyed a picnic in the grounds of the church of St. Mary. A perfect way to spend an afternoon, after which we spent the rest of the day napping in my room. I awoke to strange sounds across the lawn. And then I saw them. Like rats from a sewer they came, first one, then two, then three, then four. I left her sleeping and waited by the door. Their footsteps stopped outside the door just as I was putting on my sash. I left my pistol on the bedside table. I opened the door before they could knock. The last thing I saw of her was the moonlight on her face, pale and latticed from the frame of the window. I followed them out of High Down and into the gardens. I remember the chill against my skin despite it being summer and the earlier heat of the day. I thought it strange at the time.

If I was to say that they treated me with kindness, it would make me a liar. I prayed only that they would make it quick. They did not. I thought I heard a noise from the window of my room and hoped with all my might that she had not awoken. I looked at the darkened glass but could not see. Please be sleeping. Please still be sleeping.   I kept my eyes on those darkened windows for as long as I was able. Even as the moonlight glimmered on the sword that hovered above me, even then, I kept them open.

And here is where my story ends. And so, I will see you again in this life, or the next. My own, my love.

***

Of course I did. Of course I did. I knew he was the one from the very first moment I saw him. I knew it by the way he stared absently into space whilst smoking his pipe after dinner, as if his head was somewhere else entirely. I knew it by the way he tried to catch my eye whenever I came into the dining room and happened to be passing close to his table. I knew it by the way that he would blush when I looked back at him. I knew it by the way he would burst with pride when he showed me his sash, as scarlet as strawberries (I was less fond of his pistol, but he showed it to me nonetheless and even taught me how to load and fire it, God knows why I would need to know such a thing! I'm not sure why but it made me feel uneasy, like a cold chill against my skin, despite the heat of the room). I knew it by the way he always tried to make me smile. I knew it by the way he would brush my hand as he was passing me the menu. He thought he was so sly. I knew it was deliberate of course. I knew it by the feeling I had that I had met him before in another time or another place. But most of all I knew it by the way he took me gently into his arms and pulled my head to his chest. I knew he had other things on his mind back then, but he made me feel safe. Totally and utterly safe.

I first saw him when I was at High Down for my maids training. If I proved useful, as I was certain I would be, then I would be employed permanently at the Priory Hotel in the nearby town of Hitchin. It was here of course, that I would experience, what I would call 'true love', for the first and only time. But enough about that for now.

He called me his grey lady. I had never been called anybody's lady before, it made me immensely happy. Instead of the usual black and white uniform that was custom for maids to wear at that time, ours was a light grey and white. "*My grey lady,*" he would say. "*My grey lady.*"

It has been so long since peacetime in this once green land. To think I had moved from my parent's home in Yorkshire; God's own country, to be here, so close to this nest of political back-stabbings and warring men, fighting this time for God knows what. It made no sense to me then and makes no sense to me now. Poverty spread like a raincloud across the country. So many girls like myself had to move away from our homes to find work wherever we could. It was a dismal time. But then, as I said, I met him.

I saw him before he saw me. He was the first down to breakfast that day, and he walked into the dining room and looked considerably flustered. We all stopped what we were doing and looked at him, which only caused him to blush further. Seeing his discomfort, I pulled myself away from the others and approached his table. I curtseyed, which made him smile, and asked if he would like some coffee. His eyes gleamed with something akin to tenderness and I couldn't help but smile.

His was the first face I looked for every morning and I felt that it would be the first face I looked for until the end of time. And still, I asked every morning all the same, already knowing what his answer would be. Coffee sir? Every day I waited for his smile, for a brush of his hand. Day by day this continued, and our flirtations (if you can call them that) grew, bloomed, became more intense.

Whoever said prayer doesn't work? I was assigned to clean his room. I put fresh flowers in the vase every day, some I even picked myself. I would take my time with these simplest of tasks, giving them my utmost care and attention, lingering for as long as possible in his room. I would hold his pillow to my face all the better to smell his skin. I would spray some of my perfume on the pillows and sheets once they had been changed so that his first thought when he arrived home in the evening was of me. At least I hoped it would be.

By January our training was complete, and we were sent back to the care of the Priory Hotel. I was of course happy, but still wished that I could stay. But our story is not finished here.

I missed him intently from the very start and I would mope around the corridors and gardens of The Priory Hotel, drawing sighs and comments from the other maids. I wished he would come, why wouldn't he come? But soon enough, he did. I knew he would. I have always known it. But, it was still a huge surprise to have seen him in the dining room that first time. We caught each other's eyes immediately, and I felt the warmth go to my cheeks. I overheard him talking to one of the porters and he mentioned his room number as I walked past. I knew it was for my benefit of course. He knew that I would come to him and I knew that he knew it. Still I enjoyed making him wait. After what felt like an eternity, and after my shift had finished, I crept to his room and knocked as softly as I could.

He would come to the hotel every other day from then onwards. I knew that he also had business here so it made perfect sense. I knew not quite what he did, but I felt deep within me somewhere that it was dangerous. But all I could do was to be there for him when his worries weighed heavily around his neck. I also felt deep within me that he appreciated me greatly, although, he wouldn't always say so. We had in fact also talked about leaving here at the end of summer and being married. We both wanted to live by the sea. Something I had never seen. Truly, I sensed that one life was ending and another was just about to begin.

It couldn't last of course. Nothing good ever does. I had a day off and had gone to stay with him at High Down for the afternoon. We enjoyed a picnic in the grounds of the church of St. Mary. It was a perfect way to spend the afternoon, and I can still remember the feeling of the sun on my back. The skin on my nose and cheeks tightening slightly from the first signs of a sunburn, and my head light from the wine. Afterwards we spent the rest of the day napping in his room.

It was the first time since we had been together that when I had awoken, he was not there. I reached over to his side of the bed and I could still feel the warmth of where his body had just been. There were noises in the gardens. I stood up and wrapped a blanket around my shoulders. From the window I saw them, four in a circle, with him in the middle. I balled my fists and banged on the window. For a moment I swore he looked straight at me, but I couldn't be sure that he truly saw me. Still, I held his gaze as his head left his body and he slumped to the ground at their feet. I was motionless for what seemed an eternity and then the ground gave way beneath me.

I tried to carry on the best I could, but as hard as I tried I couldn't get over him, couldn't forget the way he looked at me in his last moments. The other maids cajoled me along and cared for me constantly. I must have been such a burden to them, but how could they understand? How could they ever understand? I was light, lifeless. I felt that I could walk through the walls if I'd had a mind to. Not quite a part of this world anymore. Who would want to stay? What would be the point?

I held his pistol in the pocket of my apron and felt the weight of it through the fabric. He had left it in the room, and now I understand fully, that he had left it for me. It all made sense now – it was as if he was always trying to tell me something. He knew how the story was going to end and he was trying to say goodbye all along. Yes, the only thing left for me to do was to destroy myself. I would do so looking through the window at the spot where he fell. I imagined his eyes on mine as I put the pistol to my head and slowly squeezed the trigger.

And here is where my story ends. And so, I will see you again in this life, or the next. My own, my love.

M C Egan

Induction

Camilla showed up ten minutes after me, making her twenty minutes early. The unease I'd been feeling for the last hour, the tightening in my chest, lightened just a little.

"My first night," she said. "Everything takes longer the first time."

"Yep, there's a lot to get through," I agreed.

"I'm Rhona. Pleased to meet you."

Camilla was only going to work one night each week – Sundays. I guessed she had a full-time job somewhere else and was squeezing in an extra day here. That's her business but could become a problem if it left her exhausted or constantly clock-watching or just pissed off at everyone around her because every waking hour of her life was spent working. But on her first night she came early. A good start. For that, she can have a smile and a cup of tea.

"Induction," I said, placing mugs on either side of a little table in the staffroom before sitting down. Suddenly, a sharp buzzing rattled round the room. Camilla jolted, causing the table to shudder. She looked irritated with herself as she dabbed a tissue on some tea that splashed over the table. "The buzzers make us all jump sometimes," I said. With good reason, I thought. "Day staff will check it out. You worked in a care home before?"

"No."

"You done nights before?"

"Used to. A&E at the Royal. Full-on."

"I bet. But not anymore?"

"I've got a young family, so I stepped back. One night a week here suits me. If I stop working altogether, I'll be de-registered."

Hmmm…not desperate for the money then. If it was just about keeping her nursing registration, she could do that with the odd bit of agency work. I wondered how long she'd stick with us.

We went through the kiddie chat. She had a couple, aged one and three. My own three were grown up. While we compared pictures on our phones, I checked her out a bit more. She was only a few years younger than me. Must have started her family late. I'd done the opposite. She dressed well – very yellow, but she carried it. Expensive looking. I found myself wondering if she married a doctor. She was pretty. I'd already clocked her blue boots. They looked new. So did the hair. African but straightened and styled. I guessed she didn't use the same hairdressers I go to in

Clydebank Shopping Centre. I wondered if she'd ever been to Clydebank Shopping Centre.

I saw the time on my phone before I stuck it back in my pocket. We didn't have long and there were a couple of things I needed to tell her. But first, I covered the basics. Two levels. Residential clients on the ground floor. I'm in charge of them. Nursing clients on the upper floor. They were residents too, of course, but they needed nursing care.

"I'm responsible for upstairs?" asked Camilla.

"Yes, you do upstairs and I do down. But ultimately, you're in charge of everywhere. You're the nurse. I'm just senior carer."

"But you know how the place works. I'll listen to you."

That was nice. I wondered how long it would last. "We've got a couple of staff each but they'll all go up and down when they're needed. Liz and Gayle work mostly with me. Teresa and Durna are with you. They're good, don't worry. Both are over from the Philippines. Trained nurses but the qualifications aren't valid here."

"So the Home gets two extra nurses and pays them care assistant salaries?"

"Yep."

"But it means they can't give medications?"

Not an easy question to answer honestly. If we were busy or down staff, they certainly did administer medication. We were often busy and down staff. Poker-face time. "No," I said. "Only the nurse and senior can medicate. You and me. And only the nurse can give I.V.s and injections." I listened to myself, knowing this wasn't all true but Camilla was going to have to work some things out for herself.

This was taking too long. I straightened my back and sped through the next bits. I told Camilla that any minute now, the day nurse and senior would join us for handover. They'll give us two lists. Residents who need watching and residents we shouldn't resuscitate. We need to update our staff about these. Handover also includes updates on any incidents that day, any new residents and deaths.

I tell Camilla that after handover, she and I will head to the meds room and jointly count each resident's pills and potions. We will stock our own meds trolleys, lock them and put the key chains round our necks. Then we'll do the rounds. As it's Camilla's first night, I suggest we do them jointly – we'll do her floor first but I warn her we'll be interrupted. There are buttons and chords in every room in the building. They set off buzzers. We have residents who love those buzzers. Residents who need lots of help. Residents who are just needy.

I tell Camilla that while we do the meds, the

assistants will start making tea and toast before bedtime. Some residents have 'do not disturb' agreements in place, but these agreements are tricky to arrange because of certain legal complications – only a few of the richer residents with family lawyers have them.

Mr. McIvor, a retired surgeon, is the most recent. He locks himself in his room at 7pm with a bottle of malt whiskey and no one's allowed in for the next twelve hours unless he buzzes. He never buzzes. Most of the residents need some help getting ready for bed. Some need lots. Some are in bed all the time and need moving and changing. Some of the ones with dementia fight. Some need a lot of cleaning. A few are nearing the end. There's usually two or three empty rooms because after a resident dies it takes a while for the relatives to collect their possessions. We give them three days and then it all gets cleared.

Three days. Reminds me of something else I want to say to Camilla. Across the table, she smiles back at me. Friendly but with a dash of serious. Attentive. Very professional. Game face. It's effective. I'm reassured but I want to bring up a couple of things. I go for the easier one first.

"Before we do the meds, I'll show you the store cupboard."

"Ok."

"It's missing some things."

"Such as?"

"Rubber gloves, cleaning wipes, pads, disinfectant. Missing entirely, or if you're lucky, just running very low."

Camilla's smile disappeared. "All the things we need for basic care and infection control. Why?"

I picked up my mug and tested the tea. Still a bit hot. "Have you met Sheila?" I asked.

"Uh huh," she slowly nodded. "She interviewed me."

"Interviewed by the CEO? You're honoured. She worries about waste. She seems to think we go through too much stuff, says she can't understand it. Wonders if we're taking it home."

"Are you?"

"No. Even if we wanted to, there isn't enough. Sheila only turns up during the day but one time she was here at handover and I showed her the cupboard. There was one single box of a hundred gloves. We have six staff and sixty residents. Some residents need help several times a night and at least two staff to lift them. We have to change our gloves each time between residents. I told Sheila to do the maths."

"Did she?" asked Camilla. I shook my head. Sheila's maths focuses on something different. "But this is supposed to be one of the better homes," said Camilla. "Aren't most of the people here paying a fortune?"

It was and they did. I'd certainly worked in far worse places than this. "I'm told Sheila has a lovely big house in Milngavie," I said and Camilla's eyes flashed at Milngavie. Not in a good way. She and the rich doctor husband I'd imagined for her would, of course, also have a lovely big house in a place like that. Perhaps they and Sheila were neighbours? "Or perhaps," I said out loud, "the sector's just under-funded by the government. And I don't think 5 years of Boris Johnson will improve things!" The Prime Minister's recent election win may divide opinion in England, but if you're looking for some common ground with a stranger in Scotland this is a safe bet.

Camilla rolled her eyes at his name, which is the standard response. Then, she leant forward with the air of a conspirator and a matching low voice. "She lives at the top of the village. Sheila and her husband. Did you know her house has a swimming pool?"

"In Scotland! She must freeze her arse off."

"It's indoors. Heated."

Damn it, that impressed me! I was ashamed of myself. Camilla nodded. She felt it too. OK, I decided. It was time to tell her everything.

"Sheila's right about one thing. We do all take stuff out of the store cupboard." Camilla screwed up her face with disapproval. I was beginning to like her.

"We don't take it home. We just hide things round the building. Everyone's got their own secret stash, I'm sure. It's the only way. And then we hope Sheila sees the stocks running low and re-orders. That bit doesn't work so well."

"Where do you put yours?" asked Camilla. "Or if you told me, would you have to kill me?"

"I'll tell you but keep it to yourself. There's a little storage room on your floor that no-one ever goes into."

"Why not?"

"It's haunted."

This was the second thing I'd wanted to bring up. I sipped my tea – the temperature was about right now.

Camilla raised her eyebrows a fraction. "Uh huh."

I shrugged my shoulders. "You've worked hospital nightshift. Didn't anything strange happen at the Royal?" Camilla was ready to laugh. I'm sure lots of strange things happen at A&E. I clarified. "Ghosts, I mean."

"There were stories. I was too busy to pay attention to them. A&E doesn't give you a moment."

That galled. It reminded me of how dayshift reacts whenever we tell them about our night spooks. It's not that they refuse to believe us. They just have an image of the nightshift being paid to snooze, chat and drink cups of tea once the residents are asleep. Day staff fit the ghost stories into that image. Like, if only we had more to do – if only we were as busy as dayshift – we wouldn't have time for ghost stories.

"You'll find the ghosts add to the workload," I say to Camilla.

And then I tell her how. Two main ways. Firstly, it freaks out the staff. There are rooms they won't go into alone. One of the toilets has no windows and a light that switches off when you're on it. No, not a dodgy bulb. The light switches off. You can get stuck in there if your phone doesn't have a torch. And we have stairs on either side of the building but most staff avoid one stairway if they can help it. It's always freezing and a CCTV monitor at the top keeps showing shadowy figures you can only catch from the corner of your eye. Yes, we tried rewinding the footage. Nothing. But if you walk past the security panel at the bottom – the one where you enter the number that sets the alarm – you hear it beeping. As if someone is frantically trying to find the right code.

You find staff are constantly doing things in pairs that could be done alone, and often taking the long route to get places. It all adds up when it's a busy night.

Then I told Camilla about the buzzers. There's lots of trigger-happy residents, naturally. But buzzers go off in rooms where the residents are on end-of-life care. Where the residents are unconscious and slipping away. And buzzers go off in empty rooms. After a resident passes, we keep their bedroom door locked for three days so their possessions are safe. When the buzzers go, we need to get the key. We go in pairs. We have to check. Sometimes we find breakages. Photographs overturned. Clothes rifled through. We tidy it up so the relatives don't accuse us of anything. We turn off the buzzer and then we leave, locking the door behind us. Sometimes, even as we lock it, we hear movement from inside.

Camilla's expression stayed fixed. She took a gulp of her tea. I sipped mine. Eventually, she said, "Lots of people die here. That's a lot of ghosts."

"Most don't stick around beyond those three days. But they keep us busy while they're here."

"When will it start?"

At that moment, the dayshift nurse and senior entered the staffroom. I look up and give them a smile. Time for handover. Quietly, I lean forward and say, "Three till four. Witching hour!"

Camilla leaned closer still and whispered.

"Upstairs?"

I saw the other two hanging back, a little impatiently. I nodded. "We have two empty rooms on your floor. They were active last night." I hesitated.

"And one on mine. Mr. McIvor's."

"Empty?"

"No."

"Active?"

"Not yet." The day nurse gave up waiting and pulled a chair to our table. "We'll get back to this later," I said.

*

The clock on Mr. McIvor's bedside cabinet said 3.19am. Next to it stood a half empty bottle of 30-year-old Laphroaig. No glass. From the smell I could tell Mr. McIvor's bowels had relaxed some time ago. It smelt peaty and slightly antiseptic. Like the whiskey.

"He's been dead for a few hours," said Camilla. The buzzer in his room had gone off less than two minutes ago. We both got there quickly. I was already carrying the key. Camilla looked at me.

"You knew, didn't you."

"He came to me earlier," I said, suddenly aware of my eye contact with Camilla. Not looking away took some effort. "I was at home, sticking on some extra layers for the walk to work. I saw him. I know what it sounds like but I saw him. At the foot of my bed, his arm outstretched to me. He was a cantankerous old bastard. Rude to residents. Rude to staff. To his own family, even. But I liked him. I was sad when he started locking himself away at night. We had an understanding. And he came to say goodbye."

"Uh huh."

Camilla and I stood on either side of the bed, silent. Not for long, though. There were things to do. Mr. McIvor lay between us, eyes and mouth open. Camilla bent down, checked out the eyes and then closed them. "I'll get started," she said.

"I'll give the room a clean. Shout when you want help moving him."

Camilla felt around her pockets. "No gloves." I pulled out a couple of spares and handed them over with a smile.

Eventually, we left the room, locking it behind us.

"I don't know what I'm going to write in the report," said Camilla.

"Just say we smelt something outside and went to investigate. Sheila gets annoyed if we write the buzzer malfunctioned. It means she needs to pay a sparky to check it."

We turned and walked together down the corridor to the staff room. We'd need to phone the doctor to come and make the death official. Behind us, the buzzer at Mr. McIvor's door went off. Ahead of us, I could hear the panel for the security alarm beeping as if an unseen hand was trying different numbers. We kept on walking.

"I think I'll mention that we don't have enough gloves," said Camilla. I nodded. "I won't mention ghosts. I'll sound like a crank." I nodded again. Camilla paused for a moment and then continued. "I am a crank, but not a ghost crank."

"How do you mean?" I asked.

"I'm a disease crank. We've had bird flu and swine flu. Ebola in Sierra Leone. Vaccines and antibiotics aren't working like they used to. I really think sooner or later a disease will come along that we can't treat. It'll just sweep through places like this and wipe the residents out. Maybe the staff too."

"Zombie plague?"

Camilla laughed. "Yep, you can have your ghosts. I'll have my zombie plague. But in my report to Sheila, I'll just ask for extra rubber gloves. Achievable goals."

"Achievable goals," I agreed. "Keep it real."

Tina Cooper

The Phantom Bread Flinger

An eerie silence descended over the room. An unnatural air hung in the erm… air. There was a heavy ominousness creeping in from… oh I don't know, an ominousness was probably creeping in from somewhere, maybe, I wouldn't know, I wasn't taking any notice. I was sweeping the trillions of crumbs into a corner to be picked up with a dustpan and brush.

It was my favourite of all the jobs to be done in the bakery. To this day I love to sweep, only nowadays it's leaves and peacock poo.

So there I was, merrily sweeping away, minding my own business when a loaf of bread appeared in the doorway of the back room. I saw the bugger land. Assuming it had fallen from a shelf I propped my broom up against a wall and wandered off to retrieve said loaf. It took me longer than it should have to twig that the loaf hadn't fallen, no, it had flown. The damn thing had landed a good six feet away from the shelf it had been previously popped on.

"Surely not?" I pondered to myself as there was nobody else to ponder with.

I returned the loaf to its starting position tand gently tapped it from behind. I wanted to see how far it would go if I were to recreate a fall. It didn't go anywhere but straight down. Deciding that there was no way the loaf could have 'landed' six feet away, I had another go.

Tap tap tappity tap. The loaf landed mere inches away from the shelf.

It was then I remembered the stories.*

The new row of shops had been built on the footings of some old shops, Jack Walker's sweet shop, and an old Catholic boy's home. The boy's home had been investigated for reasons I'll not go into, but these unmentionable reasons could easily cause the odd haunting or two.

You might be wondering, why would the ghost of a young boy throw a loaf? I wonder why the ghost of a young boy *wouldn't* throw a loaf. I spent a merry few minutes playing, Can A Loaf Fly and I was twenty-four.

*story. I once heard one story that someone had been nudged by someone or something that wasn't there.

Then…

Now.

Bob Bootman

Ghost Fakery at the Bakery

One day in Tina's Bakery
Strange things started occurring
Lights were flicking
A clock loudly ticking
Ceiling fans rapidly whirring

Then came a crash
A bright coloured flash
A whizzing straight passed her ear
Something soared for a second
Or so Tina reckoned

And landed alarmingly near
"What was that? She cried
"I nearly died!"
"Something flew straight off of the shelf"
"Loaf of Bread!" She trilled

"I could have been killed!"

"I think I've just wet myself!"

Called the Boss to confess

Had to clear up the mess

He didn't believe her story

"You'd think it were true

If it happened to you

I promise, it's not Jackanory"

"I have to prevail

I'll embellish the tale

Exaggeration is what is required"

"Must've been a Ghost

I could've been toast"

The Boss laughed

And then she was fired

Nicola Warner

One Last Goodbye

Saying goodbye was something I wasn't ready for. I placed a soft kiss on the top of his head, I waited for him to whip round with his long slobbery tongue at the ready.

Nothing.

I bent down again and rested my chin by his ear, tears lightly dampened his fur, 'bye, Buster,' I choked.

***

'I don't want to move,' I huffed, 'our memories are here, with Buster, what if he's left behind?' I asked Mum as she packed the last of the kitchen utensils.

She sighed lightly, 'he will know to follow us,' she smiled, 'we won't leave him behind.'

I followed my parents out to the car, dragging my heels. I lingered by the front door and glanced over my shoulder. The sunlight streamed through the window, casting an outline of him by the fireplace. He sat with pricked ears and a tilted head, as he always did when we left the house. His eyes asking, 'am I coming too?'

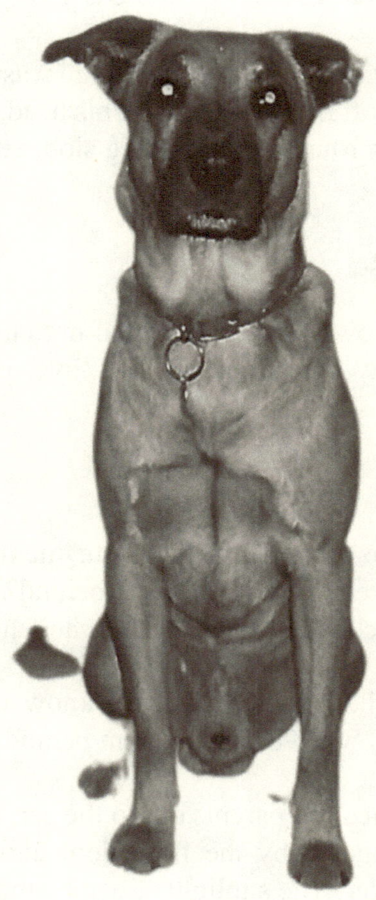

*Photo of Buster courtesy of Nicola Warner

'Come on, Buster,' I whispered, 'it's time to go,' I imagined his paws tip-tapping along the laminate as he made his way out the door, 'good boy,' I smiled.

'I told Buster to come with us,' I announced as I clambered into the backseat next to my sister.

Mum smiled at me in the rear-view mirror, 'so did I, Love.'

Our new house was smaller, but it had a cosy feel to it. My new bedroom faced the back garden, which I liked. My old room was at the front of the house. We lived on a main road, so it was very noisy, especially with a pub on the corner. There's no pub here, thankfully.

My Dad dropped boxes marked "Nicole's Room" with a heavy thud, by my bedroom window. The moving men had already brought up my furniture, placing them along various walls. I had a feeling my mum had directed them.

'Do you want anything moving around?' my dad asked, hands stuck to his hips, 'Are you happy with your bed on that side?'

I gazed at my bed with a shrug, 'it's fine there, I guess.'

'Ok then,' Dad rubbed his hands together,

'well that's the last of your boxes. Now to lug all the other boxes up the stairs, your poor old Dad. You could always give us a hand?'

I sucked air through my teeth, 'You know Dad, I would, but I really should start unpacking.'

'Well, just make sure it's tidy, you don't want your mother in here rearranging everything while you sleep,' he chuckled as he made his way down the stairs, moaning loudly about his poor old back.

I dragged one of the boxes towards me with a sigh and started to tug at the tape. The box was stuffed with bubble wrap, which I immediately squeezed, there is something very satisfying about a bubble wrap pop. I pushed the distracting stuffing aside and found my favourite picture of Buster staring back at me. He is laying upside down, his eyes bulging, and his tongue flopped over the side of his face. He did look silly. I smiled and carried him over to my chest of drawers and set him down beside my jewellery box. The perfect place for him. I can see him every time I go to sleep and every time I wake up.

I had just finished shoving the last of my schoolbooks in a box under my bed as Mum hollered up the stairs, 'GIRLS! DINNER'S HERE!'

That night I crawled to my room, my belly still full of chicken curry, rice and prawn crackers. My eyes are bigger than my belly. I settle on my bed to dive into the next chapter of Daisy Chain War.

I hadn't realised it had started to go dark until my dad had turned the landing light on, 'How are you reading in this light? You will ruin your eyes,' he scolded as he popped his head through the door.

'Ow!' I squealed, as Dad flicked on my bedroom light.

'Best get ready for bed sweetheart, no doubt your mum will be up soon to say the same.'

'Yes, she will,' Mum laughed on the landing. 'Can I still read? I'm nearly finished!' I said flicking the last two pages at him.

'Ok, but lights out, straight after.'

I shuffled into bed, pulling the duvet up to cover my ears, you know in case the vampires paid a visit. I focused on the picture of Buster staring at me, 'I miss you, Boy,' I whispered, sighing into a deep sleep.

A dry mouth and a full bladder woke me just after midnight. As I made my way back to my bedroom, I heard a jingle of metal coming from the bottom of the stairs. It sounded just like Buster's collar. Obviously, it's not, but I Zombie zoomed back to bed just in case. I pulled the duvet up a little bit higher, just level with my eyes. It's nothing. Then I closed my eyes.

There it is again.

No. That's crazy.

Go to sleep.

Then I heard light footing starting to trot up the stairs. The jingle getting louder as it made its way up.

There is nothing there.

Go to sleep.

The jingle travelled down the landing, getting closer to my bedroom door.

It's nothing.

Nothing.

My door creaked slightly as it was slowly nudged open.

I pulled the duvet up over my head.

'There's nothing there,' I told myself out loud.

The jingle was in my room.

The corner of my bed sprung, like someone had just sat on the edge and got up suddenly. Or something had just hopped on … burying itself under the covers.

This isn't real.

I'm dreaming.

I squeezed my eyes shut as the duvet rose.

Not real. Not real. Not real.

I squeezed my eyes tighter.

I waited.

Is it still there?

I breathed, and slowly opened one eye. Two glowing red eyes, stared back at me, floating in the darkness under my duvet.

I froze.

The eyes slowly turned away.

I snapped my eyes shut again with a silent whimper.

It's not real.

The end of the bed sprung as it left. The jingle clanged as it landed heavily on my bedroom floor. Soft footsteps trotted happily down the stairs. The jingle fading.

Then silence.

I hurriedly kicked off my covers and dived for my light switch and shut my bedroom door with a clunk. My heart pounding ten to the dozen.

I finally managed to go back to sleep, in the safety of a well-lit room.

'You were up late last night,' Mum stated as I stumbled sleepily into the kitchen for breakfast.

I told her what had happened with a shake in my voice and was horrified to see that she was smiling, 'It's not funny!' I cried.

'Darling, I'm not laughing. I'm smiling because I think it was Buster.'

'Buster wouldn't scare me like that.' I scoffed.

'He always got into your bed, sneaking under the covers. Then he would get too hot and jump back out to find somewhere else to sleep.'

'It did feel like him crawling into my bed.'

'He was just letting you know he was here. Nothing to fear.'

I let Mum's words sink in for a moment.

Maybe it was Buster just checking in?

It's a nicer thought than it not being Buster checking in.

Tina Cooper

Ghosts of Everything Past

I've got a new job. Hoorah. Just in time as it happens because the old one is going a bit belly up.

I came upon this job during a random conversation.

We, my mum and I, had gone to town for the obligatory birthday wander around Waterstones then on to Starbucks. It's a tradition that I started for myself a few years back. Anyone can come but I'll happily go alone if need be.

We bumped into Helen, a friend from my postie days, and as we nattered she said she was retiring. I enquired as to what it was that she was retiring from and she said she was delivering medication to those who are unable to get to the pharmacy to pick it up for themselves. The elderly, the infirm and the can't be arsed.

The old rusty cogs began to turn…

I could do that. I was a postie in a former life. I had lived locally my entire life. I couldn't be any more local if I tried. I was born for this.

This is what I told the pharmacy manager during my interview. Also Helen had given him a little nudge in my direction. The job was mine.

I was excited and mortified.

My first day was confusing and long. My second day was hellish and longer.

There was freezing fog, ice on the roads and the paths, and I got lost for 40 minutes. Me, the local postie, got lost locally. It was more than a little embarrassing.

I was beginning to question my life choices.

I'm now 6, maybe 7 weeks in and I'm enjoying it very much. It's a happy, helpful job and everyone (almost) is pleased to see me. Some folks chat, some have a giggle, some have a quick moan about the trouble they have getting a doctor's appointment and some say a quick "thanks" and shut their doors in my face. I'm happy with all of the above.

The hours are flexible and I can start when it's convenient for school runs and the like.

How lucky am I that I bumped into Helen?

I'd been feeling a tad redundant for a while, my kids were older and my services were no longer required so much. As long as they were fed occasionally they were happy but I needed a purpose.

Perhaps this was a gift to me from the universe.

Happy birthday. Here, have this thing to keep you occupied between meals.

However…

Nobody warned me about the ghosts.

They're everywhere I go.

I deliver to the Three Star Park where my grandparents once lived. I can see them waving at me when I pass. I can almost smell my grandad's apple pies and hear my grandma's strong Glasgow accent.

I deliver to the street where my bonus set of grandparents once lived. I can see them wheeling out their tea trolley full of home baked cakes and I can still remember, word for word, my grandad's favourite joke.

Women…

W wicked
O 'orrible
M mean
E evil
N nasty

Man…

M magnificent
A 'andsome
N noble

I deliver to the street where my parents lived before my dad got sick and mum moved in with us. I can see him washing his car on the drive or mowing the lawn. I can see them sitting by their pond feeding their fish. I can hear Tim, the cat they stole, say "ello" or ask for "ham" as cats do. Well, this one did.

I deliver to my old boss at the bakery where I worked when I left school. I can see my old customers. Waggy, who gave me money for ice cream when I was off on holiday even though I was in my 20s. Iris, who gave me Christmas presents long after I'd left and right up until she died. I can smell the well-used and nicotine-stained carrier bag belonging to the chap who came in every Friday for one small loaf. Each week I'd say, "see you next week", and he would return the sentiment until one week he replied, "god willing." I didn't see him the next week.

I deliver to my childhood estate where I can see me, as a carefree kid, riding my bike with Clarence (the neighbour's cat) in my basket or standing at the end of our street to watch the farmers set fire to the fields after harvest. I can see Mr Lincoln, our next-door neighbour, the first person to die that I knew and loved. After he died I would post a flapjack through their letter box for Mrs Lincoln as they were her favourite and I hoped to make her smile even if it was only once a week on flapjack day.

I have a new job.

I deliver locally and locally is where all my ghosts live on.

Paul Clark

Lost property lost again

Where do the ghosts of possessions lost go
Umbrellas, false teeth lost years ago
These spirits and ghosts of times past
Can't they have peace and rest at last?

All the offices on the railways spread
Are closing, closed but about the dead
Travelers moving amongst our streets
Swapping tales on Brit Rail's seats

All these items deserve some space
To give past souls sweet solace
They needn't be lonely or alone
A strong keep of metal and stone

Wait, look beyond the river mouth
Skylines abound between north and south
There, through the clouds it's not so hard
Let's move to move them in the Shard

*Photo Courtesy of Mina

Tricia Ramsay

Mary King's Close
In Sickness and in Health

It was October 2005 in Scotland. My husband and I were newlyweds, having gotten married less than two weeks before, in a seventeenth century Manor House outside of Edinburgh. We had spent the first week of our honeymoon in a B&B on the hillside of Loch Lomond. After a week of long nature walks and boat trips on the Loch, we were spending a few days back in Edinburgh before heading back down south to England.

The weather was not going to be the best for the next few days, so we decided we would turn into typical tourists, and book some Edinburgh tours. One of which, was Mary King's Close.

On the day, Spencer had got up early for a ten-mile run and once he was back, showered and dressed. We had some breakfast before hopping onto a bus, going further into Edinburgh towards the Royal Mile.

Mary Kings Close is situated on the Royal Mile, across from St Giles' Cathedral. The Mary King's Close is located under buildings on the Royal Mile, in the Old Town area of Edinburgh. It is the only preserved 17th century street. You can walk through a labyrinth of Old Town alleyways. It took its name from one Mary King, a merchant burgess who resided on the Close in the 17th Century. The close was partially demolished and buried due to the building of the Royal Exchange in the 18th century. Then later, it closed to the public for many years. The area became shrouded in myths and urban legends, tales of hauntings and murders. But it was reopened in 2003 for tours.

When we got there, we had to line up with a group of others waiting for the tour to begin. We got a brief health and safety talk with our tour guide and then we started to descend two floors beneath the Mary Kings Close gift shop. The first thing you notice is how much warmer it is down there, compared to above ground. Quite a few of us took our jackets off within a few minutes of going down. There is lighting, but you still need your eyes to adjust at first. Then the tour began, with our tour guide dressed as a person from that era, apart from him carrying a walkie talkie which was the only form of contact and communication with the staff above ground.

The living conditions were not great, but for those who were from higher standing, they had the advantage of living higher and closer to the ground level, as some of these buildings had several floors. Those who were poor would live down at the bottom of the building in cramped, disgusting, and squalid conditions.

As we continued to walk around, I noticed a sensation like my jeans were being tugged. At first, I ignored it, then when it happened again, I tried to see if anyone was close to me, who might have accidentally brushed past me. Or a buckle of someone's rucksack may have snagged at my jeans. There was no one close enough, not even Spencer. As the group started to move, I deliberately held back so I was not too close to anyone. As the guide finished talking about the people who lived there, and what their jobs were, we started to move onto the history of the plague.

When the tugging happened again, I can only say I got the impression, because of the height of where my jeans were being tugged, it was that of a small child when they are trying to catch an adult's attention. Tugging at my jeans at the outside of the top of my thigh. In my mind, I said "ok, thank you, I know you are there", and it stopped. Then we moved again into a larger room where people who had the plague, had been taken and left to die. Only family members who had survived the plaque would visit, bringing food and trying to care for the afflicted.

The room was dark with cobbled flooring. There was a made-up bed from the 17th century with a dummy in it to demonstrate what the poor, sick people would have looked like. With boils on their skin, their face looked in pain. Some of those who had been brought here and left, had been children. They even had a made-up dummy of a "quack" Doctor, in full length leather coat and a beak like mask. The uniform helped the physician prevent direct contact with the bodies of plague victims. The beak-like nose of the mask was filled with aromatic herbs to filter and purify the air breathed by the plague doctor to prevent contagion.

That's when our guide announced he was one of those people who used to care for the sick, as he had survived the plague but most of his family had perished.

Spencer was standing next to me.

"I don't feel good," he said.

I looked at him and told him to lean against the wall. Before I knew it, he was sweating and looked like he was about to pass out.

"Help me," I shouted as I grabbed one of his arms and a guy near grabbed hold of his other arm.

"Watch his legs," I said as they buckled. We wanted to get him on the floor without him injuring himself. The guide stopped his talk and came over. I told him what had happened, explaining Spencer had no medical conditions. The guide grabbed his walkie-talkie and called for assistance.

Gradually, Spencer was coming around and we managed to get him back on his feet as the second member of staff came over and helped to get us back up to the surface and the group tour continued.

We sat Spencer down in a chair in the gift shop. The assistant got him a cup of water from a water dispenser. Spencer said he felt boiling hot but he was shivering. His T-shirt felt damp to the touch and his skin was clammy with sweat. We sat there for a few minutes whilst he sipped his water slowly. Once he was feeling more himself, we intended to head towards the exit, but he decided he needed the Gents before we left. Whilst I was waiting for him to come back out, still holding his coat, I saw a guy I recognised from our group, he saw me and walked over.

"How's your partner?" he asked.

"Oh, he's ok now thank you, he's just popped to the loo. Has the tour finished?" I asked.

"No, I kept feeling something was touching me. Pulling at my clothes. It freaked me out, so I came back up early."

"Oh, that happened to me too, I just told it, I knew it was there and it stopped."

At which point the guy physically shuddered like someone had walked over his grave.

Spencer came out and walked over.

"Glad to see you're feeling better," the guy

said before he walked away from us.

I explained the conversation I had had with him as Spencer put his coat on before we walked back out into the busy Edinburgh Street.

"So how are you feeling now?" I asked.

"I feel better than I did but I still feel a bit weak, drained," he replied.

I had a quick look around and saw there was a coffee shop just a bit further down the road. We crossed over the road and continued towards it, weaving through the crowds. Trying to find somewhere to sit was not easy as the place was heaving. I came back with drinks and a sandwich for him to eat. Now normally Spencer is a bit of a health freak, being a runner, but I just looked at him, "don't turn your nose up at that bacon and egg roll. It was all I could find, just eat it. It will give you a bit more energy," I said all matter of fact.

I sat down next to him and sipped my coffee thinking about what had happened, then laughed, "I know I said, 'in sickness and in health', when saying my wedding vows, but I didn't expect it to kick in this quickly," and smiled at him.

A few years later, I saw a ghost hunting TV show called, *Most Haunted* and it visited Mary King's Close. Their medium came over funny in a room and had to be taken out before he came back around.

When I checked, he was in the same room with the bed that we had been in when Spencer had his funny turn … coincidence?

I also found out there was a room where people say they get their clothes tugged at and they believe it's the ghosts of the children who had been left there and had died from the plague. The most famous of those was a girl called Annie. Tourists leave cuddly toy gifts for the children. But we never saw that on our trip as we had to leave before we got to that point of the tour.

Paul Clark

Trails in Time

There's a ripple in the hedgerow
Alongside the byway dark
Apparently legions march tonight
Dog spectres growl, hark

Was that a spear catching a dogwood twig
Perhaps the rustling of greaves
A shield catching its neighbour
Or the crunch of autumn leaves

Does every life leave a shadow
We pick up these vibes and sounds
A pike mark or a bullet
In many battle grounds

History is written by victors
But third Richard was made whole
A search made in a car park
Cleansed his mortal soul

These past voices send their clarion call
Pause in these holloways
Take in the scents and sounds
Listen, listen, remember us always

Find us in the half light
In village and towns' streets
Beneath the veneer of wood and stone
Your ancestors you'll meet

We're not here to harm you
We're not here to scare
Our history is your history
Show us that you care

MC Egan

Jitterbug

I hadn't realised the date was important.

A couple of weeks earlier, I'd written the words 'MEET JOSIE – ST ENOCHS 12 NOON' on the Scottish Castles wall calendar stuck to the side of my fridge with masking tape. The calendar was a present from my wee sister Josie. The same Josie whose name now occupied the 6th June box. It was the only entry for the month and, in fact, any month.

I kept catching myself staring at the scribbled appointment. I'd be going for milk or peanut butter or beer but then I'd stop and just stand there, eyes directed to the side of the fridge. Sometimes I would look at the big picture of Clackmannan Tower. June's castle. I'd never heard of it, was unlikely to pay it a visit and thought it looked menacing even in the sunshine. Finally, I remembered. The sixth of June. A year to the day that I had last seen dad alive.

It wasn't the day he died. That was easy to remember. Of course, it was Christmas Day. Josie even predicted it months earlier with a grim joke about how ruining Christmas had always been a special talent of his. And he would have loved the irony of George Michael dying the same day. Mum had always loved George. But Dad was conscientious about not letting her have anything – not even George

– so he took her old 60-minute cassette of songs she'd taped off the radio when she'd been at school. He kept it in his sock draw and whenever he took it out and put it on, it was his way of saying things would become physical. He ritualised it. Side A meant mum "just needed a wee reminder." Side B was "serious." Sometimes he played the whole tape. A serious reminder.

Meeting at St Enoch's Shopping Centre was Josie's idea but she wouldn't have known about the date. She'd been badgering me (again!) to leave the flat. I said, "I do leave the flat," and of course she knew that was true. I just didn't leave it enough or go very far. She worried about me. I should go into town and meet her for lunch. On a weekday, when it isn't too busy. Sober. She kept talking. I didn't follow it all and it didn't matter. She was looking at me with those kid sister eyes. Tears were forming. I had no choice. I grabbed a pen and went to the calendar.

I planned the day. Not obsessively. Ok, a wee bit obsessively. I just wanted everything to go smoothly. I would bath and shave that morning. I would buzz what was left of my hair to a number one all over. I would wear my newish clothes and make sure they were washed three days before so I could hang them up on the bathroom rack to dry and lose their creases. Three days to dry out. I did the same for myself. I let the fridge run out of beer and hopefully the money I saved would pay for Josie's lunch as well as mine. Sober was hard but not as awful as I'd imagined. I needed to be normal when I met her. I would not smell. I would not look strange. I would not slur or stumble. I'd just be one more person out there and no-one would notice me. There was a bus stop outside my flat but I didn't want to deal with the driver, so I would walk to Partick station and get a ticket from the machine. St Enoch's underground was right next to the Shopping Centre. I would get there early. If it was very busy, I could hang back until a table was empty. By the time Josie arrived, I would be seated. Unflustered. Ready to do lunch with my wee sister.

I shoe-gazed my way through Partick without incident, save for the odd dog shite. A couple of minutes later, I was rattling about on the half-empty tube train. Parts of the tunnel had a sewage smell and as it seeped around me, it brought back memories from a year earlier.

I was in dad's flat. The short walk from hallway to living-room was a riot of smells: unflushed toilet, booze, smoke, grease, vinegar and sweat. And there he was, on that black, leather reclining chair of his that none of us would ever in a million years dare sit on. A rash of red and brown spots where his hair used to be. His once neat beard just grey scraggle. That body of his, built for violence, now withered into nothing. I could probably have picked him up with one hand but instead I stood there hoping to God he wouldn't see me tremble. How did his eyes stay so bright? As though all the malicious energy that once flowed through him had retreated and concentrated in those two points.

The tube doors opened. Leaning over, I could just make out 'St. E' on the wall. A couple of old boys in the carriage got up and shuffled out. I followed. On the platform, I heard a wheezy laugh from one of them and smelt tobacco.

My dad's eyes. I kept seeing them. He had looked me over and asked why I was there. He was not polite about it. Because he was dying, I told him. That kind of honesty would have got me into trouble back in the day. Now he just sat glaring at me, thinking of something poisonous to spit my way. "Where's your sister?" Yep, that would do it. No way would I talk about Josie with him. She had a life of her own. He didn't get to share it. Not one tiny bit. "Tell her…" I felt my fingers clench. Still giving the orders! "Tell her she needs to come see me." Palpitations stuttered up my throat from my chest. I couldn't speak. I could shake, so I shook my head. The look he gave me, yet I defied him so meekly you would laugh to see it. As I turned to go, he found the funny side. He cackled till he choked. The sound followed me out.

I stopped on the underground platform at St Enoch's and let the old boys walk some way ahead of me. Something about their wheezing laughter and the smell of cigarettes made me hang back. "A wee reminder," said a friendly voice through the speaker.

"Please don't smoke until you are outside the station." Outside the station, the two old boys were busy lighting up, coughing at the first draw. In the rain, St. Enoch's Square looked grubby but today the sun seemed to clean it. Glass shop fronts flashed at me. Some of the younger men had their tops off, displaying grey, wiry bodies. Women wore short skirts or loose flowery dresses.

Josie was right. It wasn't so busy on a weekday. The entrance to the shopping centre was there. Through the corner of my eyes, I saw a security guard watch me. He held a walkie talkie to his mouth – it was big and plastic like something from an earlier decade. I tried not to hurry past him. To the left, the ground floor of a toyshop. Dead ahead, escalators to the first floor where all the other shops waited. Folk were coming in and out of the toyshop. Mostly grannies and toddlers. They go to play with the toys for a while and then leave without buying anything, or so I'm told. But one girl cuddled a new fluffy monkey in a stripey T-shirt. A long time ago, I clutched a monkey of my own. One of the few toys I'd been given. I called him Bobopher Christie - don't ask me why - and I loved him. I must have stared at the girl. She stepped closer to her mum as she window shopped. I looked away.

I pictured Bobopher Christie in dad's bedroom, standing in the corner, facing the wall like a naughty schoolboy. I'd been afraid to admit to something or other and dad decided to blame

Bobopher until I owned up. I was too scared to own up. So Bobopher Christie stood in the corner of dad's bedroom for weeks and weeks. Then, one day, he vanished.

"We get rid of bad monkeys."

That voice. I stopped at the foot of the escalator and looked behind. A young couple nearly walked into me; the man looked angry. Neither of them spoke. It was an old voice. Not the voice of an old man but the voice of a man from the past.

On the first floor, I struggled to find the second set of escalators. Really, I just needed to pay attention to where other folk were heading but it took me a while to realise that I'd been unconsciously avoiding the busier parts of the Shopping Centre. Eventually, I found myself once more moving smoothly forward and upwards. I smelt hot fat and vinegar, as the sandals and shoes of shoppers on floor two rolled into view. Carefully scattered across the hall, I saw glossy red tables with benches bolted to the floor. Along the walls, fast food chains surrounded us with brightly lit logos in primary colours. It wasn't quite lunch time yet but the place was already filling up. A couple of empty patches lay across the way, so I began to weave through tables and people. The girl with the monkey grabbed one of the free tables so I sped off at a tangent – trying not to look obvious about it. I reached another bench I could claim.

"That's my chair."

That voice again. I stopped in my tracks, took a deep breath and looked round. I couldn't see the speaker but people kept catching my eye as I scanned the room, forcing my gaze back down to my feet. I felt a pain in my side and I realised I was clasping myself.

Jitterbug…Jitterbug…

Wham! Through the food hall's hidden speakers. Only it sounded like someone was messing with the volume. My legs suddenly ached and I felt self-conscious just standing there next to the empty table. I moved to the other side and sat down. Side B of mum's tape. The first song. I would sit in the bedroom I shared with Josie, my fingers in my ears, while it played. It's funny what you memorise. I remembered all the distortions in mum's radio recordings. The way the songs grew louder and quieter at different points. The way certain notes fuzzed and cracked.

I sat listening in the food hall with each anticipated flaw in the song compressing my chest like the twist of a tourniquet. I pushed a tear from each eye as I closed them and slid cold fingers in my ears.

"Open your eyes," said dad.

I stopped breathing.

"The Devil if I have to tell you again, boy. Open your eyes!"

The blackness I saw would not be still. It flickered and winked but I kept my eyes shut.

"Be a man."

I shook my head.

He exhaled through his nose with a snort. Then, "You're meeting someone."

I paused. Then I shook my head again. I thought about opening my eyes. Then I felt something brush against my cheek.

He would do that. He would lean close up, his huge, square face in front of mine, and he would brush his thumb down my cheek, close to my mouth. I could almost taste the sharp, sweet reek of tobacco-stained skin.

"You can tell me the truth, boy," he whispered. "I've seen you piss your knickers more times than you can count. I know when you're hiding something."

I scrunch my eyes and press my fingers into my drums. But I keep hearing him.

"Josie's coming, isn't she."

I shook my head.

"You brought me to her."

Under my eyelids, a flash of white panic. Is that what I was doing? Yes! Josie got away. She built a new life of her own, a good life, against all the odds. I was her only reminder of what happened before. I was her only link to dad.

"Open your eyes." A sudden slap to the side of my face. Without thinking, I snapped my eyes wide open.

There he was.

He was young again – younger than me – and he had that odd sense of being two different people stitched into one. He was your mate - confident and friendly, working you with a look here, a smile there. But he was someone else too - someone packed brutally tight and ready to rupture. I'd seen both sides – the friend and the foe. I knew which was the real deal.

He leaned close, his eyes pressing hard on me. "When she comes," he said, "tell her she needs to remember me. Tell her it's time to let me back in." He pointed to my forehead. "In here." Then to my chest, to my heart. "And here."

And at that moment I saw her.

She'd got there ahead of me and I hadn't even noticed. It was the girl with the monkey that threw me – made me look away. It must be Flora. I hadn't seen her since she was a baby. For all Josie loved me, she never brought Flora along when she called on me. Not while I was drinking. I knew better than to argue – Josie had seen what men do with a drink inside them. She drew a line. It could not be crossed.

But without realising, I drew one too. A line that can't be crossed. I was never as brave as Josie. I'd spent too long with my eyes closed and my fingers in my ears. When I got older it only got worse. The awful feeling that I should be a man. That I should be standing up to him. Protecting my family against him. But I couldn't. I just couldn't. Yet despite the shame and the guilt and the self-loathing – despite all of that - even I had a line. He would not get to Josie through me, and he would not - not - not get to Flora.

"No."

I stood. Something shifted as I rose. A wall. A barrier. In my head and in my heart. I looked at the other table. The table with my sister and niece. I refused to glance down at the seat opposite me. With my head firmly up, I joined my family.

Flora must have decided in advance that she wanted a new uncle. God only knows what I must have looked like and she had no memory of the last time we met. All the same, she told me to sit next to her. When I did, she held out the monkey.

"She spotted it in the toyshop," said Josie, "and made me buy it for you."

I took the monkey. Not crying was hard but I didn't want to scare Flora. "Thank you," I managed.

"Mammy said you used to have a monkey, Uncle Jamie. With a funny name."

"Bobopher Christie," I nodded. I spoke to the monkey. "He disappeared but I think I can call you Bobopher Christie Two."

"Is he like the monkey you lost?" asked Flora.

"Not really."

"Then you should give him a new name. I'll help you if you like."

I smiled at Flora. "You're right," I said. "He's a new monkey. Whatever name you choose will be perfect."

Bob Bootman

Until I See it…

Never seen an apparition
Or sighted any spooks
Not taken up by Aliens
With extra-terrestrial looks
I've not had a close encounter
Of any sort of kind
Never have been hypnotised
And no-one's read my mind
Not going up to heaven
Or even down to hell
I am a non-believer
I think that you can tell
I'll stay that way forever
Until it happens to me
Then I can tell the stories
Of the strange things that I see

Mina M

Ghostory

Going on a ghost tour has been fun. We made jokes about ghosts lurking around Hitchin town, some with no head attached to them, some holding a fish (weird) and others robbing the place we went for a drink at the end of the tour. The guides tried to mix history with ghostory to make it more interesting. I even tried to die by stepping out into the road in front of a car as a way of experimenting to see if I could reappear as a ghost. Nicola heroically saved me and Tina wisely explained that even if we die now it might take a century or longer to appear as a ghost and haunt the shit out of people. Lewis who was using Bob's ticket was expected to play Bob and make us laugh. Well, he tried.

A tiny crescent of moon with its small entourage of stars was hanging on a far corner of the sky which funny enough added to the spookiness of the environment. It was a crisp and cold night and on the way back to the car park we all felt the cold penetrating through coats, gloves and hats.

Once in the car, I turn on the heating and await the much-desired warmth which never materialises.

Usually it takes only a few minutes for the car

to warm up but tonight it just blows an icy cold breeze through the ventilators. I am forced to turn the whole thing off and wrap my coat around me and drive as fast as is allowed (maybe a bit faster).

I find it weird that there are no lights on at home. They must be very tired to have gone to bed so early. I enter the living room in search of the usual roaring log fire that has been on every night this winter. Well, something is on but instead of the usual cheerful red and orange, silverfish blue flames are dancing around my wood burner. Strange!

'Didn't you know ghosts prefer the cold?' petrified with fear I can't even turn around to see the source of that frosty voice. I feel movement around me and a misty cloud of rustling silver inches forward and positions itself in front of the mantel piece forcing me to lift my eyes and face it. I gape as my eyes rest on a beautiful, perfectly proportioned face of a young lady. She is not very tall but her erect body and her long, puffy dress make her look impressive. Her long hair is tied up at the back of her head and covered with a bonnet. A glamorous lacy shawl is covering her shoulders. Even though everything on her looks shimmering silver, I can distinguish or maybe guess the real colours she is wearing. Her dress is dark green velvet. Her petticoat is of light brown, the same colour as her boots. Her hair must be very light gold and those shiny, cold eyes are certainly grey.

'Am I dreaming?' I finally manage to mumble

not taking my eyes off her face.

'It really depends on how you want to perceive it.' Her speech is slow and measured. I don't see a smile but I have a feeling that she is mocking me.

'Who are you? Why am I talking to you? You are not a ghost are you? Why am I even asking? Of course you are not. There are no such things as ghosts.' I go on ranting, looking at her, looking around my unrecognisable living room, blinking hard and trying to wake up. She doesn't interrupt me. Simply stands there looking and waiting for me to process my feelings of disbelief and shock.

After a long while she finally decides to put a stop to my raving and says, 'Where are my manners? It's most unladylike traveling atop your moving box and barging into your home without even introducing myself.'

I look at her perfectly arranged hair and her neat attire wondering if she really has been sitting on top of my moving car only moments ago.

'I am Lady Charlotte-Deborah Grey, residence of the Priory House in Hitchin. I believe your honourable guide called me Lady in Grey tonight. It goes to show how much is lost in history. I never liked wearing grey.' She sighs heavily as if getting her fashion style wrong was equally as grave as distorting many other historical events.

'Would you like to take a seat?' I feel sheepish for offering a ghost a seat in my home but what is the etiquette in such a strange situation? She nodded politely and moved towards the sofa gently lowering herself on the edge of the seat keeping her back straight.

'I don't mean to be rude but what are you doing here in my house or in my dream, maybe?'

'I heard you say that you wanted to write about me. So I thought I could help you print a more authentic picture of me.'

'What? Were you there in the hotel, listening to our conversation?'

'I was just passing by. I was on my way to visit Lord Havisham in his room upstairs. Poor man, he is pretty depressed tonight.'

'Is that the one with the fish?'

'Oh, for the love of God, will you people drop this nonsense about fish?'

'Ok, ok, sorry, so you want to help me write about you. Don't you think there are better writers to get your story done? Take Lewis for example, he is an excellent writer and he is very interested in ancient history. Or Nicola, she is from Hitchin and knows the history better than me and I think she believes in ghosts.' Lady Grey doesn't reply for a while, instead she intensifies her frosty glare as if to study the contents of my mind.

'I am sure your friends are all fantastic writers, but you are the one who said you wanted to write about me and with such an army of ghosts marching around you I thought you would understand better.' She circled an elegant arm around my living room as if to prove her point. Horrified, I follow her hand half expecting to see armed ghosts standing to attention.

'What army of ghosts?'

'As your guide mentioned tonight, ours was a romantic story.' Totally disregarding my question and ignoring my mortified state, she tells her story.

'They told you my lover was dashing handsome, and that he was. I met Capitan Goring at an evening dance in the town Hall. As usual my dear husband left me with a group of young girls waiting to be invited for a dance and went off to play cards with his older friends. I was only seventeen and newly married. Lord Grey was many years my senior and had already passed his dancing days. He brought me to such social events to give me an opportunity to meet other local ladies and make friends. Being shy by nature I found this task very hard to muster and ended up quite lonely and uncomfortable in times like that. The men were all standing on the other side of the room sneaking looks in our direction, wondering perhaps who to invite for a dance.

Goring was standing quite alone in a corner. I thought he too was new to town and felt a certain kind of affiliation with him. Later I found out that the other men didn't approve of him being a cavalier and avoided his company. Was it fate or love at first sight or whatever else the romantic writers call it these days? I do not know but for me it was simply the warming ray of sunshine that I had been deprived of by being forced into a loveless marriage. We danced all evening, most of it on the terrace and away from the crowd. We even snuck into the dark alley to exchange a few hot kisses. I desired him, longed to bed him and to be with him all the time and so without any hesitation agreed to meet him secretly the next day.

Our secret love affair went on for five months, transferring me into a happy, well satisfied and confident woman, which my husband interpreted as me settling into my marriage. Settling, however, was out of the question for the majority of the population of the country those days as we lived in the most unsettled times. The country was on the brink of a civil war and stories of atrocities and mass killings travelled around shaking our little bubble violently at times.

My Goring and his small group of royalists were constantly harassed and assaulted by the parliamentarians who called themselves roundheads. The beautiful golden hair, which I lovingly combed for him every time we met, was a political statement that he carried around and infuriated people with. I begged him to let me cut it for him. I promised that I would still love him as much, but he insisted on wearing his political beliefs atop his head. He said it was cowardice to hide what he believed. Finally, when he was forced to go into hiding, I offered my attic and managed to keep him alive for forty-five days.

It may sound pathetic, but those were the happiest days of my life. Each morning as lord Grey left for his business, I sent the maid out on some errands and spent a couple of hot steamy hours in the attic in the company of the most amazing man I had ever met. My world shrank into that tiny space in my attic and I did not miss the big outside world. Serving him, looking after him, even emptying his chamber pot was more satisfying than attending glamorous parties which I gladly cancelled under the pretence of headache and colds.

As the saying goes, all good things must come to an end and our tragic end came much sooner than expected. It must have been the maid or another domestic worker who informed on us and my enraged husband sent men to drag my poor helpless cavalier out of hiding and into the side street.

I sobbed uncontrollably as I was held by my husband, forced to watch my lover's head being decapitated. I don't want you to think I was a royalist. They were not any better and I didn't want to take sides. I have seen many changes in the ways of society over these past centuries and almost all those changes have been made from rivers of blood.

You, I am sure understand me because even though I don't know you from all those young ghosts around you, I gather you must have seen your fair share of violence in your life.'

'You freak me out Lady Grey. Tell me what ghosts? What are you talking about?' I follow her hand gesture around my empty room once again and look back at her. I want her to leave. I want this nightmare to end. At the same time I am curious to find out if she really sees something or someone.

'My poor heart couldn't take the strength of my sorrow. The prospect of life without him was so dark that I passed away less than a week after his death.'

'Stop there please. I am sorry to hear about your tragic end but you have to tell me what you are referring to when you say army of ghosts. Or else leave my home, because seriously my heart can't take any more of this and I don't want to join you and Capitan Goring haunting people in Hitchin.'

'Did you know that ghosts are nothing but segments of memory?'

She doesn't seem to register the urgency in my voice or pretends not to anyway, 'How can it be? You lived in the 1600's. I haven't heard of you until tonight. How can you be a segment of my memory?'

'Just like the living, some of us become icons or household names as they are called these days. Due to the political and social situation of our time, Goring and I became household names and stayed on in people's memories being passed on from one generation to the next. Most often people imagine seeing us because they have either read about us or heard about us. That's how the human mind works.'

What she is saying is a piece of rich philosophy or science and I need time to digest it. She allows the silence to go on for a while not taking her penetrating gaze off my face.

'I do sincerely thank you for listening to me and trust you to write something good about me. And also please forgive me for making you uncomfortable.' She stands up and glides towards the door.

'Wait, wait. Who do you see here?' this time the hand gesture is mine and she does bother to take her eyes off mine to follow it.

'I will say my farewell and let you have a moment with your friends.'

As she evaporates from my living room the warmth returns and my log fire is once again dancing red flames. I am sitting on the armchair in front of the fire and yes as she has been saying I was completely surrounded by an old but familiar crowd. They are all there, smiling and nodding at me. Some reach out to touch me; others wave or blow me a kiss. Rather than being terrified, I feel content and safe. I am with my friends. I look at their dear faces that unlike mine have not aged and are still glowing with youth.

Kobad is wearing his full gear, turning his bazooka ammunition belt around his fingers as if playing with some prayer beads. I can even smell the multi layers of perfume he used to wear. Kazhal is still wearing her hair shoulder length. Mohsen is standing tall and lean in front of the fireplace, while Kamal is humming his favourite song about the girl with a beauty spot on her cheek.

'How I miss you all.' I tell them tears streaming down my face. They shuffle around. Move in closer and try to console me.

'I feel guilty for being alive all these years, for enjoying a happy life, having children, traveling around, seeing the beauty of the world. It is not fair. You should all have been here and done the same.' I reach out to touch Kobad's hand but my fingers only curl around thin air.

'You must stop feeling guilty. We died fighting for a better world and we are very proud of it.

It was just by luck that you didn't join us but

that is ok and we are happy for you. You need to let go of the past so you can enjoy life better.'

I am not sure who is doing the talking. It seems to be done collectively which I found really strange. But then again, what part of all this was not strange?

'I love you.' Is all I can say as I see them leave, one by one, smiling and waving goodbye.

Bob Bootman

Para-un-normal Activity

Imagination is incredible
Think of all the dreams, you dream
Wake up in the morning
Think how real they seem
Your mind, it can play tricks on you
What you want to see, you see
If you tell yourself you've seen a ghost
Then that's what it will be
Alcohol might play a part
Once you're drunk, you're drunk
Many sightings happen in old pubs
That theory, we can de-bunk
If ghosts were real, they would be nude
Cannot go from undressed, to dressed
Some ghosts seem very dapper
Clad in their Sunday best
Always one that looks like Shakespeare
Headless in a ruff, that's rough
Roman Soldiers or a murdered child
I think I've had enough
Nice to think we return when we are gone
But when you're dead, you're dead
I won't be re-appearing
No matter what you've said

Joe McDermott

Keeping the Hitchin Ghosts Alive

I must start by stating I am cynical when it comes to Ghosts and Paranormal activity, but I love a good yarn as much as the next person, and as a writer and member of the Creative Writers Club, I am always on the lookout for a great tale that I can make my own. And that is why I found myself and several of my fellow budding authors booked onto a "Ghost Tour of Ye Olde Hitchin Town" as an assignment to gather inspiration for a series of ghostly short stories for a future book release.

Earlier on that night my partner had roped me into joining her on one of her online Tarot Card reading sessions. We all have our weaknesses, mine is Italian Football. Hers are supernatural messages from the beyond.

So I joined my partner on her laptop in the office, her the eager believer, me the nonchalant cynic and a couple of clicks later we had joined her weekly on-line Tarot reading with her physic Crystal Destiny. This is obviously the modern take on séances. No sitting round a table with dimmed lights and holding hands here. Shame, there was little for me to ridicule.

Crystal wasn't dressed as I expected, all in black with Goth make-up. Facing us on screen was a normal middle-aged woman dressed in a lilac sweatshirt, with her hair wrapped up in a scarf.

"Hi everyone, thank you for joining, I've got a good feeling about tonight, there have been several spirits near me all evening".

We watched on mute, while several of the other women online were contacted before she says hello.

"Joe, welcome. Hello Jasmine" (my Partner). "Jasmine? I'm getting a message about a chip on your favourite Mug. Does anything like that resonate with you?"

"Hi, no not really," Jasmine replied. It's obviously our turn.

Crystal shuffles her Tarot deck several times and turns over a top hat and places it face up on her table. She looks very puzzled and shuffles the Tarot deck again several times and a card jumps out from her hand as if it's been flicked.

Another top Hat. "No, No, No, NO!" she says in a slight panic. "I don't have Top Hats in my Deck. One of my kids must have been messing with them earlier, I'm so sorry Jasmine."

"That's ok," Jasmine replies. It's then that she notices a chip on the lip of her mug, her favourite one with a picture of her cuddling her cat, the love of her life.

"Oh bugger, look at that," she says.

That's my excuse to leave. "I'm off to my writing club darling, we're going on our Ghost walk in Hitchin tonight." I kiss Jasmine on her forehead and grab a coat and scarf for the night. It's been quite a mild week for mid-February, but it's best to wrap up.

Anyway, back to my review of Sunday Night's Ghost Tour of Ye Olde Hitchin Town.

I park in the Car Park by the duck pond in front of St Marys Church. The book club have arranged to meet by the War Memorial in Churchyard Walk where the Tour is due to start and as usual I'm the last to arrive. Everyone's there except Hailee our Tutor, I've got her ticket. She's meeting with a publisher tonight to arrange the next release dates for our books to get published.

As if by magic, we are soon surrounded by other couples varying in ages. There was 8 of us and now there was a small group of 20. The evening has grown chilly suddenly and a light mist has appeared. I'm glad I've brought a scarf with me.

"Good evening everyone." I turn to see two Gentlemen step out from the dark shadows under a streetlamp which appears to be shimmering. It's all very theatrical. They are both dressed in long grey cloaks and dark, dusty top hats. One has a silver topped cane while the other carries a rolled-up newspaper in his gloved hand.

They introduce themselves as Andreu and Derech (a bit old fashioned or European I reckon) and they explain they have been citizens of Hitchin for many, many years and have now long retired and do these Ghost and Historical tours as a hobby to keep them out of mischief. Cue lots of polite laughter.

Andreu holds out his arm and opens an old-fashioned pocket watch in his palm and explains that as it was Sunday tonight this was to be a Ghost Tour and that it would be approximately 90 minutes and snaps the watch's cover shut.

The other members of the Book writers club have come well prepared, equipped with head lamps, infrared torches, night vision goggles and even a divining rod, but unfortunately none of these accessories will be needed this evening.

Our tour starts by entering the graveyard of the resplendently lit St Marys Church and we gather opposite the Church's main entrance and our guides explain the history of what St Andrews church was originally and how it became what we now know as St Marys.

Before them are two gravestones unexpectedly engraved with skull & crossbones which did not depict pirates, sailors or vampires, but possibly victims of a plague. Several other tombs are described, but sadly, graveyards were not a good hunting ground for ghost sightings, so we were to follow our mystical hosts in their ancient apparel as they strode briskly by the shops in Churchyard walk and they suddenly stopped at the mouth of Hunts Alley. Here they revere many tales of ghostly apparitions seen to have either entered or passed through the alley down the ages, mainly dark shadows, but that was probably poor lighting along that stretch. We progress single file through the alley at a brisk pace and I notice it was a lot colder in the alley than in the open street.

We doubled back down the High Street, stopping at the Cock Inn where Andreu informs us of several ghostly sightings of women, often in "50 shades of grey", smelling of lavender or how the presence of male ghosts was often predicated by a noticeable smell of burning wood or tobacco and how male ghosts were always depicted wearing ancient apparel (as worn by our guides I noticed). The smell of Lavender featured a lot in their stories but I surmised this could be explained by the fact there was once an old Lavender Distillery located in the centre of town.

Derech then chips in with many sightings of ghostly black cats, especially as dark blurs on modern CCTV, and he explains that the burial of cats in the foundations of buildings was once a common custom in the 18th century to ward off Witches.

The old Pubs and Coach Taverns were a source of many reported sightings and tales. We break off at the Red Hart along Bucklersbury where there's often a sighting with a modern twist of a biker roaming the streets in his jeans and leather waistcoat often seen opposite an infamous old motor bike repair yard which was once located there.

While there, Andreu tells us "The Red Hart inn is a natural place for a ghost to linger, as it was said to be the site of the last public hanging in Hitchin," to minor gasps from the group and open eyed-looks at each other.

Derech recounts, "Mrs. Shepherd, a trainee manageress, recalled one night being awoken by a sense of cold in her hotel bedroom, and saw the shadowy figure of an elderly man sitting in an ancient armchair only a few yards from her bed."

"I was not afraid," she said, "adding that it added character to the place."

We giggle and move on.

Outside the Hitchin Priory we are told the best story of the night. There was a definite air of expectation and build up for this one. Dating back to the 14th century, the legend has it of a headless horseman, Yes! This is more like it.

Andreu recites, "It's believed to be that of Captain Goring the Cavalier, a royalist killed by Roundheads during the civil war while he was visiting his mistress, a maid working at the Priory. She is often sighted wearing a Red cloak. And on certain summer nights the ghost of the Captain and the clatter of his horse's hooves on the cobbles can be heard and often seen galloping up and down Tilehouse street in his desperate attempt to flee his parliamentarian captors. He's easy to recognise, as he doesn't have a head!"

We next muster at the Sun Hotel, "Dating back to the 16th century when it was a traditional coaching inn, it is reputed to have several ghosts haunting the place including Lord Havisham, who committed suicide there and he is often seen hovering along the corridors and in particular room 10, which is no longer available for hire after multiple unexplained accounts of patrons feeling an unwelcome presence in there".

Derech recalls the stupidity of some grave robbers who one night tied up the landlord of the Sun and liberated the many guests in the bar of their purses at the end of their flintlocks, before fleeing with their loot. Unfortunately they were witnessed earlier that evening carving their initials into the Inn's archway, and so it was quite easy for the Sheriff to identify the individuals and round them up to be duly hanged. It was reputed they can often be seen haunting the bar area! Although I think spirits of another kind are probably the root cause of these sightings.

"But not all ghost sightings are scary", Andreu continued. "In the eighteenth century, two clergymen, Mark Hildesley and Edward Young, were in the habit of playing bowls together on the green behind the Sun Inn and crowds would gather to watch them play. They clearly enjoyed their games so much that they continued the practice after death, and the clink of bowling balls and voices can sometimes still be heard."

The tour was coming to its conclusion and we headed back towards the car park by St Marys and our final destination is the small park at the entry to Biggin Lane, where our guides inform us that during the Back Death this area was known as Dead Street and was a warren of small streets and slums with no sanitation. The plague wiped out the whole community of several thousand people and the area is still thought to consist of several plague pit burial sites.

And our last tale of the evening is based upon the site of the old Dead Street School, during the typhoid epidemic of the 1850s where the sad story of Mary Biggins (of whom the lane is now called) was recalled. Mary would beg with her young son outside the school and she was soon to tragically "inflict upon herself an ending resulting in her unfortunate demise" due to the circumstances of her desperation, destitute and inability to provide a future for her young son, she sadly killed herself.

Suicide was considered a mortal sin and her body was never interred in a Christian burial ground, but where the streets crossed so she could not come back to haunt the town. Her sacrifice, however, was intended to benefit her son. He was taken into the nearby Alms housing, but unfortunately there was to be no happy ending, he did not rise up to become the future lord Mayor of Hitchin, but it is said the ghost of a young boy is reported to be seen wandering the corridors of the Alms house searching for his mother.

And with this sad final tale our tour had ended.

The gathered crowd applauded for an enjoyable evening spent walking around the Medieval town. The Writing Club huddled and agreed it was time to find a pub to warm up and re-cap the evening. It had gotten considerably colder in the last few minutes and I could see my breath visibly as we talked to each other and could now also get the pungent smell of burning tobacco and wood, as if there was a bonfire close by.

I turned back to give my thanks. Andreu and Derech were no longer there, and spookily the other members of the tour had also vanished, it was just the book club. Where our guides had just stood, there was now an old weather-beaten headstone bearing an engraving with two top hats tilting towards each other with an inscription in an olde worlde script:

"HERE RESTETH THE CADAVERS OF BROTHERS

ANDREU AND DERECH DRAUGHER

HISTORIANS AND WARDENS OF HITCHIN'S UNEARTHLY SECRETS

WHO GAVE THEIR *ENTIRITIE* FOR MANKIND AND THIS WORLDE

IN LIFES PERPETUAL CONFLICT BETWEEN GOOD AND EVIL"

Draugher. Why was that word familiar?

It was then I remembered, Drauger! That was the name given to a supernatural spirit or a ghost used in the Netflix Viking series Last Kingdom.

By the headstone the rolled-up newspaper lay like a bunch of flowers left there by a loved one.

I picked it up and it was cold and brittle to the touch. I carefully opened it and it was an old copy of the Hertfordshire Mercury, a local newspaper which I don't think had been printed since 1921. There are no pictures on the front page but the headline took me by surprise:

Heroic Hitchin brothers killed in terrifying paranormal episode.

It was dated 23rd February (which was today).

But for 1873.

Paul Clark

Do They Really Go Bump in the Night

Do they really go bump in the night
I don't think that's actually right
A marsh bound Will O the Wisp
Creeps up on you with a lisp

Now a djinn coming in makes a din
Hopefully he'll go straight after he's bin
Making wrong uns quite madly
Is a skill I'd have gladly, but, no sadly

A spectre is a silent sort
But deep down he's a sport
He'll always allow an escape track
So carry a silver sword in your backpack

Don't try to fool with a ghoul
They have no sense of humour at all
Just grab what you can and sprint
Don't stand your ground like Clint

Spooks have fallen out of favour
Men in suits or geek breakers
Try to ignore their white covers
As you would the dune avid lovers

Tricia Ramsay

Saying Goodbye

I stared at the time showing on the side of my computer screen. It had just gone four, I had another hour and a half before I could clock off from the office for the day.

I had been distracted all day. For some reason I kept replaying our breakup which happened two weeks ago. Daniel and I had been together for two years and I had become quite close to his family, my outlaws. To think I had once thought we would end up married. How naive of me, after knowing what I knew now about Daniel's secret addiction. It made me chuckle, but not in a humorous way. More in a resentful way, as the only alternative would be to cry and I didn't want to cry anymore, not in the office.

I took a deep breath and then tried to refocus on the screen before me, but it was no good. Maybe going for a quick walk to stretch my legs and give my eyes a break from the screen would do the trick. I got up from my desk and carried my coffee mug over to the kitchen area and made myself a fresh cup of coffee, then sat back down. As I did, I noticed a new text message on the front screen of my mobile.

It had come from "him" and produced a sickening feeling in my stomach. That instant rush of adrenaline, which just aided my sense of nauseousness. I quickly took a sip of my coffee before picking up my phone and opening the text. This was the first time he had made any attempt to contact me.

Beth.

Come over to the flat once you've finished work this evening. Bring your keys in case I get caught up and end up running late.

We need to talk.

Dan

My place of work was local and it would only take me fifteen minutes drive to get to our flat … correction, his flat. That's probably why he's asked me to come over, to hand the keys back to him. It would have been easier to pop them in an envelope and push it through his letterbox, had he not said he wanted to talk.

As I drove, I put the local radio station on as background noise, whilst replaying that night again in my head from two weeks ago. When I had confronted him about his behaviour and strangers turning up at the flat I didn't know exactly what was going on, but I knew he was lying to me. Even when I gave him every opportunity to come clean he wouldn't. His pig-headed stubbornness wouldn't allow him to. I know you have to be hard skinned to work in finance in the City of London, but I was his girlfriend. He should have been able to be honest with me. I wasn't going to let this slide, I know my worth and if I didn't challenge it, that would be my downfall further down the line. What kind of a future would that have been. SO, I had to end it. Even though it broke my heart, I couldn't live in this lie.

It turned out he had been partying a bit too much. He had an addictive personality and had addictions from gambling and being in a lot of debt to cocaine usage. I know I made the right decision and I just hoped he was not going to make things difficult.

As I was parallel parking, I heard the radio announcer cutting in. "There are delays on the trains tonight due to an incident earlier this evening. Trains have been stopped from Potters Bar and buses have been laid on to help commuters get to their destinations tonight. We will keep you updated with any additional news as it comes in."

I finished parking, switched off the engine, locked the car then looked up at the flats. I couldn't see any lights coming from the flat. He's probably going to be late if the lines are up the spout tonight.

I entered the building and walked into the lift to reach the 6th floor. Taking the keys out from my purse for the last time, I opened the door and let myself in. The flat was in darkness and it felt cold. I walked from the hallway straight to the kitchen and put the kitchen cabinet's down lights on, so I had enough light to see the kitchen worktop. On auto pilot, I turned to put the kettle on to make a coffee... old habits die hard. I walked over towards the table and stopped suddenly, screaming out in shock. There was a figure seated in one of the chairs.

"Sorry, I didn't mean to startle you Beth." I couldn't see him very well because of the lighting but I recognised the voice.

"What the hell are you doing? You nearly scared me out of my skin. Why are you sitting in the dark?" I walked towards the main light switch, to rectify the situation.

"No stop! Don't put the light on, I've got a banging head. I think it's a migraine," he said.

I turned around to face him. He was still in his work suit and looked tired. I came back to the table and placed my coffee down before sitting down. "Why did you want me to come over?" I looked down at my coffee.

"I wanted to apologise. I really messed up, didn't I? I never meant to hurt you or allow all this to get out of hand. I'm sorry I wasn't honest with you.

But what has happened has happened and I'm righting the wrongs, I have made," he sighed and his eyes seemed to drift off as if he were seeing something, which wasn't there.

"Dan, I know about the gambling and drugs," I confessed and went to reach out to touch his hand, but he flinched away.

"Please don't be nice and understanding. I really don't deserve it. I'm so sorry and if I could turn back time I would, but I can't." He looked around the room. "I'm going to lose this place to pay off the majority of my debts. I spent the last week trying my best to keep my job. I can't see myself getting any bonuses this year or promotion. Did you know HR wanted me to grass up other employees who are doing drugs, can you believe it?"

"I'm sorry you're going to lose this place, we had some fun happy times here, didn't we?" I said with a grin. "But I'm glad you're working things out," looking at him, "it's cold in here, do you not want to put the heating on?"

He looked like he was in pain as he was rubbing his forehead.

"Are you ok? Have you taken anything for it?" I asked. The thought crossed my mind, he might be having withdrawal symptoms from his drug use.

"No, I think I just need to have a lie down

soon, to rest, ' he replied, and I knew it was my cue to leave. I took the flat keys out of my jacket pocket and went to hand them over to him.

"Just leave them on the table," he said.

"OK, I'll head off, but I hope you feel better soon. Thank you for apologising to my face, it means a lot." I stood up and walked towards the kitchen door.

"Beth, do me a favour, promise me you will find a man who's worthy of you, who treats you right. Promise me you will love again and be happy in your life."

This was a surprise coming from him and it caught me off guard and I could feel tears welling up in my eyes. "I will. Goodbye Daniel."

I got back into my car and the radio came on. As I was driving back home, which was now back with my mum, an up-to-date news report came on. They announced the reason for all the problems with the trains. There had been a jumper, some poor sod had jumped in front of a train earlier that evening. They identified the person but would not release their name until their next of kin had been notified. I decided to take a detour and get a takeaway before getting back to Mum's and once I was in, she came out of the sitting room.

"Where have you been? I've had Gloria on the phone wanting to talk to you. She seemed ever so upset. She asked me to ask you to call her once you got in. It seemed important. What's Daniel done now?"

I looked down at my mobile. Six missed calls. Funny, I hadn't noticed it before. I thought I'd better give her a quick call. Gloria was Dan's mum and she had always been nice to me. The phone rang for a while.

"Hi Gloria, it's Beth."

"Hi Beth, it's actually Stella," (Dan's sister) she seemed upset "I take it you've heard?"

"Heard what?"

There was a sharp intake of breath on the line.

"Oh, it's Dan, he's gone."

"What do you mean gone? I …"

"Dan took his life. This afternoon, he was the person who jumped under the train, which caused the problems with the train service tonight."

My head was spinning. "No! this can't be true... WHEN?" All I could squeeze out.

"The police said it happened around 4:30 this

afternoon."

"I'm so sorry Stella, I've got to go." I got off the phone. I scrolled back through text messages and to 4:28 but when I tried to open up the text it wouldn't open. I burst into tears. My mind flashed back to what Dan had said to me last at the flat.

"Beth, do me a favour, promise me you will find a man who's worthy of you, who treats you right. Promise me you will love again and be happy in your life."

That was him, saying goodbye.

*photo courtesy of M C Egan

M C Egan

Rowan, the Haunted Tree

Have you seen Rowan, the haunted Tree
In Kirkintilloch Cemetry?
Next to the grave of Anne MacVie,
Mother and Grandma, ninety-three.

Look at him blush when he flowers in May.
He's a redberry pom-pom by Midsummer's Day
He waits for October. He's longing to say
To the Autumn wind, "Blow my leaves away."

Here stands Wee Annie, by the grave of her Gran.
She likes to say 'Hiya' whenever she can.
But old Autumn Rowan looks gnarly and wan.
All twisted and bare, like a Bogeyman.

The clouds have got darker, the day becomes wetter.
Wee Annie wants shelter but will the tree let her?
No, he won't! Rotten Rowan is out to get her.
He swings a sharp branch and rips Annie's sweater.

Looking down, Ghost of Gran sees Wee Annie
sadden.
She eyes Rowan up with a scowl like a mad 'un
She whispers, "That tree, right there, he's a bad 'un.
He'll be sorry! Tonight, it's…armagaddon!"

Granny Anne, you might think, was not much to look at.
A chubby wee ghost in a bib-bobbly wool hat.
But she raised twelve weans in her wee cobbly, full flat.
And you just don't mess with a Gran who has done that!

That night, Rowan sees, as his bark goes all clammy,
The light of the Moon reveal something uncanny.
Ghostly Gran rising up from the ground for a rammy.
"Don't you dare scare my Annie, you nasty wee…."
GRANNY!!!!

In a fury, she shouts "You're too big for your roots.
So I'm telling the lightning clouds 'Take aim and shoot!'
I'll be fetching my boys with their chainsaws and boots.
When I'm through, you'll be nothing but cinders and soot."

Rowan knew she talked true from her fevery pitch.
Grannies get what they want. They've got leverage.
"No please No!," he whined so. "I'll stop being mean.
I'll grow back my leaves and become evergreen."

So now all year-round Rowan looks like a pom-pom.
Always nice to Wee Annie, coz he's scared of her mom's mom.

Bob Bootman

Footless Ghosts

If you've ever seen a floating ghost
Why can't you see their feet?
And even more confusing
Where did they get the sheet?

Nicola Warner

Through the Veil

Grace beamed excitement as bubbles fluttered in her belly. Her dad helped drop the Veil over her face, as she stood in front of the double doors to the ball room of the hotel venue, 'if you're going to cry, now's the time, just make sure you dab your eyes before you see Jake,' her dad winked at her as he creatively positioned a square of tissue into her bouquet. She giggled at him compensating for the Maid of Honour role her sister had no interest in, instead she was balanced in a squat in front of a door handle, trying to apply lipstick.

The classic *Wagners Bridal Chorus* sounded as the double doors opened. Not her first choice, she wanted to walk down the aisle to *a thousand years*, she loved that song. But no, tradition triumphed. Grace took in a deep breath, releasing it slowly as she began to make the journey towards her husband to be, gripping her dad's arm.

Jake smiled with a glint in his eye as he watched his bride. He felt his chin almost buckle under emotion. He cleared his throat and puffed out his chest. Their eyes met as she joined him at the altar, he melted her with a crooked smile.

They had only been together a few months when Jake proposed. Grace had thrown out the word 'yes' so fast it took her by surprise. The most spontaneous thing she had ever done. Her family weren't as supportive at first, 'Oh these whirlwind romances never last, love,' her great-grandmother told her. Their wedding day was filled with similar comments, 'no one thought this day would come.'

Jake shook his head at them, 'the only thing that could keep us apart would be the old grim reaper!' he laughed.

***

She watched helplessly through the organza mist that now separated their worlds. He hadn't moved. He sat in his favourite armchair, clutching their wedding photo. They were so much younger then, her flawless skin radiant in the glorious sunshine, her eyes glistened with bliss. He ran his finger slowly over the apples of her cheeks. He glanced every now and then to the empty chair beside him. His eyes welling as he did. A glass of water, half empty still rested on a placemat on her side table, waiting for her return.

'Grace, you know you shouldn't watch the grieving, you're not strong enough to comfort yet.'

Grace felt a tingle round her shoulders as her Mum wrapped her energy around her. Oh, what she would give to feel the warmth of a body-to-body hug.

'Look at him mum, he's broken.'

'He's grieving. It will take him some time.'

'Why can't I pass through this?' Grace held her hand out over the organza curtain; static snapped a warning.

'Your energy needs to build up before you can pass through. You need to grieve too.'

'How long will that take?'

'It's different for everyone sweetie. I've seen some take months, others years, and a few, only days.'

'I can't bear to see him like this.'

'All the more reason not to watch the process, my darling.' Grace felt a surge brush over her face.

'Why is no one with him?' Grace moved closer to the veil, staring at the corded phone, urging it to ring.

'Come with me Grace, there are many waiting to see you.'

As her mother, guided her towards a glowing tunnel she turned back to the veil, the image of her husband slowly fading, 'I love you, Jake,' she whispered.

'Gracie?' he muttered back, his eyes breaking from the photo in his hands.

'Did he just hear me?' Grace gasped as they reached the end of the tunnel.

Her mother stayed silent as she opened a chromed wooden door. A spark shot out towards them, and danced around Grace, before darting off again.

'Still has his zoomies,' her mother laughed.

'Max?' Grace awed as she watched her childhood pet as a ball of light bounce up and down the limitless white space, just as he did around their living room whenever someone returned home. It was his ultimate display of affection, 'where are we?' she asked as the bounding ball rested.

'We come here to greet friends, family … pets, as they come to terms with their passing. Pets are a little easier to comfort, as you can see.'

Grace looked around at the room filled with balls of light, some big, some small, more flashing in as other doorways opened.

'Why didn't I come here first?' Grace asked.

'You were pulled straight to Jake, Darling. It happens sometimes when death calls unexpectedly.'

'How did I -'

'Let's not talk about that now sweetheart. Look.'

Grace turned to see glowing orbs behind her, as they moved closer, she could easily make out their features, 'Dad?' she cried. His energy pulled around her.

***

It's been three days. Grace had promised she'd keep her distance from the Veil until she was strong enough, or to at least gain enough energy to withstand the snaps of the static drape. She couldn't stay away any longer. She needed to be with him. She needed to know he was coping.

Grace had been taught the technique of travel. Although she had yet to travel to a person, she had been practicing with places. Surely, it works the same way? She was confident she could get to him. She closed her eyes and pictured his face. She felt a strong jolt pushing her forward, leaving her just outside the veil. She squealed to herself, 'I did it!'

Slowly, she approached the Veil. It was clearer. Like looking through heat rising from the radiator in front of a window. She raised her hand. The static fizzled quietly.

'Gracie...' she heard Jake whimpering.

He wasn't in his armchair, which she found bitterly comforting. At least he was moving about.

'I need you ...'

'I'm coming!' she called back, knowing full well he couldn't hear her. Squaring up to the veil she pushed out her hands. The veil spat angrily at her, but determination took over. Her hands broke through the Veil with a crack. It felt weird. Like the pins and needles you get if you lay in a funny position for too long. It didn't hurt, so she carried on moving. Pins and needles ran through her arms and travelled through her body inch by inch. The veil snapped and hissed at her. It reminded her of the static cling you get when you separate clothes out of the tumble drier. The veil pulled her back, snapping and fizzing, clinging to her leg like a chunky knit cardigan refusing to let her go. Grace threw herself forward, and with a loud snap! the veil released her, hissing its annoyance.

As she backed away from the Veil she was taken by surprise when she found her reflection in the mirror, 'this isn't right,' she frowned as she touched her face. She looked ... young ... not as young as she did in her wedding photo, there were smile wrinkles round her eyes and her face a little rounder, your face changes, doesn't it? But she wasn't... *old*.

'Why, Gracie?' she heard Jake's muffled cry. She dismissed the mirror and followed his sobs.

She found him. In their bedroom, curled up in a ball cradling her pillow. He looked so tired. He was just as handsome as the day they married, even with his bloodshot eyes framed in dark circles. He hadn't changed, but men don't seem to age do they? If anything, they get younger. Don't you just hate that?

Grace moved towards the end of the bed, 'Jake?' she said softly, 'I'm here, Jake.'

Nothing.

She sighed, 'Why can't you hear me?'

'We needed more time ... we still had time,' he cried into the pillow.

'Oh, Jake,' she whispered.

'Gracie?' he shot up, eyes scanning the room, 'Baby, are you here?'

'He heard me again!' she squealed out loud, 'I have to whisper,' she told herself, *why the hell didn't anyone tell me that?* She positioned herself on the bed beside him, 'Jake, I'm here. I'm with you.' She told him softly.

A smile flickered, he let out half a laugh, 'Jesus Christ, I'm going mad...' he said as he rubbed his hands over his face.

Did he not hear me? What am I doing wrong? She looked at him, tears rolling over his cheeks and resting between his lips. Slowly, she lifted her hand and cupped his cheek, trying to wipe away his sorrow. Her hand started to glow over his face.

Jake moved his hand through hers and held it there for a few seconds, closing his eyes, 'I am going mad!' he snorted to himself.

OK he felt something then. He's getting flustered.

Flopping himself back into his pillow, Jake ran his hands through the curly nest on his head. She loved his curly hair. Every Friday night they snuggle on the sofa to watch a film, always her choice. He'd place his head in her lap and she would twiddle his curls round her fingers, letting them spring back one by one. He would be asleep within 10 minutes. What she would give now to sit beside him and run her fingers through his hair. She watched him as he sighed deeply, his eyes drooping.

There must be some way of reaching out to him, she thought. Grace remembered something she was told as a child; *your mind is most open when you dream. Maybe that's it? Maybe now is the time I can reach him.* She shuffled closer, rested her hand over his chest and leaned into him, placing her mouth against his ear, 'Jake? Can you hear me?'

'Uh huh,' Jake mumbled.

Yes! Okay let's not get too excited, that could have been a fluke, 'Jake? It's Grace.'

'I miss you Gracie,' Jake muttered.

He answered me. Not a fluke, 'I'm right here.'

'Don't leave me.'

'I'm staying with you. I will always be with you.'

Jake sighed with a smile and slowly opened his eyes.

Grace smiled back at him, it felt a bit silly knowing he couldn't see her, but it was just a natural reaction.

Then his face dropped … 'Gracie?'

***

Jake double blinked and rubbed his eyes, exhaling loudly, 'I thought I just saw …'

The doorbell rang, making Jake grab hold of the alarm clock, 'shit.' he cursed to himself and stomped heavily to the front door.

'Did you get any sleep?'

It's his mum.

'A little. Weird dream though... Grace …'

'Well, that's a hell of a lot more than I've had. I don't mind helping you out Jake, I really don't, but I've done my time of hourly feeds. I'm too old for this now.'

'But-'

'I'm sorry if that's selfish or insensitive, but I can't, I need a break. And this little guy needs to bond with his daddy.'

Daddy?

'But I don't know what to do! Not without Grace.'

'I will show you the basics, while I'm here. It will see you through the night. I just need some sleep,

Jake. Go get showered and changed. I'll sort him out in here.'

Grace moved closer to the little cherub, fast asleep in his car seat. He was the double of Jake, dark hair, olive skin, even the chin dimple. She cooed at him ...and then it hit her. Pain ripped through her stomach.

'Grace!'

Grace turned slowly towards her mother. Despair etched on her face.

'Darling, come back through the Veil, I will help you through this.'

Grace floated slowly to her mother, stopping just before the border, 'you should have told me.'

'I couldn't.' Her mother explained, 'you had to figure it out for yourself. It's part of the rules.'

'How could I just forget I was pregnant? Why did I think I was old when ... it happened?'

'Trauma, Darling. We experience it the same way. Come back through, we can work through it together.'

'No.' Grace turned to watch Jake's mum cradle and comfort the newborn. Something she should be doing, 'I'm staying here.'

'I understand, of course I do, but Darling, the longer you stay on that side, the harder it is to come back through. You will lose your charge.'

'I'm not a battery!' Grace huffed.

'It works in the same way. You need to build up energy on this side to be able to pass through the Veil to that side. If you don't bring your energy charge back up, you could get stuck.'

'Wouldn't be the worse thing to happen.'

'Maybe not now, no, but eventually. Just promise to come and see your dad and me?'

'Maybe. I need to help him do this.'

***

The first night was the hardest to watch. Jake sobbed. The baby wailed. He paced the length of the living room, doing the bounce the baby technique that his mother had shown him earlier. The baby tired himself out and settled long enough for Jake to crawl onto the bed and close his eyes. Screams erupted from the tiny bundle.

'For someone so tiny, you've got a good pair of lungs, boy,' Jake sighed. He looked at the time and then at the feeding notes his mum had written. He left the baby in his Moses basket and went to make a feed.

Grace stood over the baby, shushing him softly, telling him he was in good hands, 'go easy on Daddy, little one,' she whispered.

Jake returned shaking a bottle, 'ok little dude, let me just test this out for you,' he said, shaking a few drops of milk onto his wrist, 'ah I've got no idea, it's not hot, so ...' Jake put the bottle on the side table and scooped the baby out of the basket, settled on the bed and offered him the bottle.

The baby suckled hungrily at the teat, his face damp with tears.

'That's better isn't it, little man?' Jake smiled, 'I can't keep calling you Little Man, can I? You need a name...' Jake pondered, 'now your mummy would have suggested something like Jake Jnr, or something daft like that,' he chuckled.

'I would not!' Grace scoffed.

'I've always wanted to be called Bruce.'

'Oh dear god, please don't call him Bruce!' Grace begged.

'Nah, I don't think mummy would like that one either ... what about Harry... or Liam ...?'

'Now you're just going through One Direction ... but Harry, I do like Harry. Put that on the list!'

'I have a feeling mummy would approve of Harry.'

'Seriously! I'm sure you hear me!'

Jake sat the baby up gently, and started rubbing and patting his back, 'oh your mummy would love you. I bet she's here, watching ... judging.'

'I am not judging!' Grace shouted, 'I think you're doing an amazing job!'

'I'll make sure you know her, Harry.'

'Ooh we're going with Harry?'

Jake giggled, 'I'm sorry Gracie, I can't. I can't call him that. All I'll think about is Harry Styles!' The baby promptly let out a deep burp, 'see Gracie, he doesn't approve either!'

'Well, that was rude!'

'Do you want any more of this buddy?'

'The elf? Oh dear lord, please, no!'

'No? OK. Let's change you then and put you back down?'

Grace watched with blurry eyes as Jake carefully removed the bottom half of the baby's sleep suit and gave him a fresh nappy. What she would give to share this moment with him, and every moment after. This was as good as it was going to get, but at least, this way she could share some part of their life with them.

When Jake dozed off, she whispered into his ear how proud she was of him, what a great father he was and that Harry was a great name, but also threw in some other options, Ezra, Harrison, Joey and Zack.

Jake laughed through his nose, 'I'll think about it,' he mumbled.

***

'Gracie?'

Grace turned to the veil and slowly walked towards the voice of her husband.

'All this time?' he asked her, 'you were right there?'

Her eyes filled as she stared at him through the organza mist. His crooked smile, his misty blue eyes, the dimple in his chin. It was him. Just as he looked on their wedding day.

'I can't pass through,' she told him. Static snapped as she raised her hand over the veil, 'I'm so sorry I wasn't there to greet you.'

'I know. Your mum explained things to me. You can pass through though.'

'No, I can't. I never went back. I soaked up every minute I could on this side.'

'Gracie.'

'Yes?'

'You can pass through. Take my hands.' The veil crackled fiercely as Jake's hands broke through, 'take my hands,' he told her again.

Grace gently placed her hands into his, he gripped them tightly. She could feel the pulse of energy between their palms. He pulled her towards him and she flew through the Veil with a pop! No angry crackling, no static cling.

Jake pulled her into his arms, 'I've waited a lifetime for this,' he whispered to her, 'we can watch over Zack together, you don't have to do it alone anymore.'

Bob Bootman

Recurring Nightmare

There's banging on my bedroom walls

Tapping on my door

Increasingly I'm worried

What do they want me for?

Hear shrieking and then howling

The rattling of a chain

Shouts of desperation

The screaming starts again

They're crying and then wailing

They're calling out my name

Try to get inside my bed

Every night's the same

I need to get some proper sleep

Close my weighty eyelids

Wish I could turn back the clock

Not had these bloody kids!

Dominic Hatley Aged 11yrs

World's End

WARNING: if you get nightmares please do not read. Thank you. Enjoy.

I heard a noise from the loft. It wasn't a rat or a bat. I wondered what it could be. Taking a hammer, I stepped up the ladder Dad had left in the hall then opened the loft hatch, only to see … nothing. Nothing was there. Not even a speck of dust. I went back down wondering if I should do anything else as it had been the strangest of noises but it was getting late so, eventually I simply went to bed.

The next morning. I woke in a happy mood, only to be disturbed by the noise again. My smile disappeared like a scared poo. I can't even explain what the noise sounded like exactly. It was just … a noise. I took charge of my hammer once more and strode up the ladder. Lifting the hatch this time was again met with … nothing … but as I went to close the flap I saw a note on the floor.

I watch you all the time but you can't sea me.

First of all I thought, wow what bad grammar. Then, I couldn't see anything. Almost as if there was a bag over my head but no one was there. When my eyesight returned and I could finally see again, I was somewhere else. My feet hadn't moved from the ladder, aside from almost toppling backwards when I saw the note but now I was sitting in a chair. My hands and feet restrained. There were four ghosts surrounding me. Staring. Their eyes burning into me like the sun on a summer's day.

I whispered, 'W w what do you w w want with me?'

They failed to respond.

Continued to stare.

After around ten minutes of silent staring they said, 'We want to know all of your countries secrets.'

Confused and exhausted I blurted out, 'You're stupid! If you really want to know all our countries secrets, why do you want an 11-year-old who just wants to play fortnite?'

They responded quicker this time, 'Good point. Help us get to your Leader.'

I sighed. 'Urrgh fine, but only if you get me 10,000 v bucks.'

They agreed.

Nice doing business with you ghosties. They seemed quite annoyed but it was worth it. First stop, number 10 Downing Street. The ghosts made us appear in the property and slammed a door in front of us open. Turns out we went into Rishy Sunak having a bath.

Sunak convinced the ghosts to head for the white house and aim bigger than just the UK.

Once we arrived in America we stormed in to get Joe Biden and the ghosts and I legged it to a mysterious place. Once there, Joe was pressured into sharing all the facts he knew about the world. Then they refreshed his memory, let him go. Gave me my V Bucks, let me go. All seemed normal.

One Month later…

You might think a month after giving ghosts top secret world facts, not much would have changed. LOTS CHANGED. Whilst ghosts were shooting nuclear bullets, I was on Fortnite buying Wenagade Wader.

And that's the story of how an eleven-year-old ruined the whole world.